Francis Henry Underwood

James Russell Lowell

A biographical Sketch

Francis Henry Underwood

James Russell Lowell
A biographical Sketch

ISBN/EAN: 9783337170653

Printed in Europe, USA, Canada, Australia, Japan

Cover: Foto ©Raphael Reischuk / pixelio.de

More available books at **www.hansebooks.com**

JAMES RUSSELL LOWELL.

JAMES RUSSELL LOWELL

A Biographical Sketch

BY

FRANCIS H. UNDERWOOD

BOSTON
JAMES R. OSGOOD AND COMPANY
1882

CONTENTS.

LIST OF ILLUSTRATIONS.

JAMES RUSSELL LOWELL.

A BIOGRAPHICAL SKETCH.

THE essence of poetry eludes analysis, and
like some of the forces of nature is known
only by its effects. These effects are so various that any uniform standard is impossible.
At times poetry lurks in satire and in images
of the grotesque; sometimes it swells in the
fervor of religion or of patriotism; sometimes
it creates for itself an interior world, as the
Inferno or the Paradise Lost; sometimes it
expresses emotion in view of the beautiful
or the sublime in nature; again it shines in
pictures of human life, as in the Canterbury
Tales or the Arthuriad; or it unfolds the
mysteries of the soul and touches the universal analogies, as in Shakespeare.

1

Since the time of Wordsworth, poets of the English race have been strongly influenced by natural scenery. The poets of old made *man* the subject of verse. Virgil wrote like a modern of woods and fountains, but in this respect he is alone. Homer knew the blue Olympus and the wooded Ida, and Horace could behold the snowy summit of Soracte from his Sabine farm; but all the " scenery " in the classical poems of antiquity (excepting the Æneid) would not make a page of a modern magazine. We have been having in our time a surfeit of landscape art, as in Wordsworth himself and in his followers, including Bryant and other Americans. Many modern poets have been scarcely more than literal scene-painters, and have neglected to put human figures in the foreground.

Poetry reaches the soul through the intellect and through the emotions. Purely intellectual poetry may be in a sense " classic," but it has no life. Poetry makes men feel, rather than understand, and it suggests thoughts and emotions not expressed in words. As History is only ceremony and costume until genius connects it with the vital interests of the race, so the most artistic landscape is only a vapid picture of still-life until man appears in it, informing it with his own hopes and fears.

Poetry, in its essential quality, is disengaged from the products of the ordinary mental faculties. It is something wholly apart, not a summary nor an epigram. It never expounds, comments, nor exhorts. It teaches, if it teaches at all, by what it suggests, by subtile hints, and by apt parables. It is only a truism to say that poetry is the highest and rarest of the productions of mind. But few poets are wholly poetical, or " of imagination *all* compact." Some dross is fused with their gold. The temptation to discuss is very strong with men who live and bear their part in the world. And it has generally happened that great poetical conceptions have been born in loneliness or in darkness.

The subject of this sketch is one of the most favorable examples of English descent and American culture. As he was born in a time of ferment, both as to literary and theologic dogmas, he was naturally influenced by the revival which the early part of this century witnessed. He has profited by the literatures of all nations, but he has been the disciple of no one literary master. His success in verse is fairly matched by his brilliant and poetical prose; and while he is eminent among scholars, he is at the same time capable, discreet, and distinguished among public men. The events of the times in which he has lived, and the changes that have taken place in his own sphere, as will be seen hereafter, have affected in various ways the productions of his pen.

PARENTAGE AND FAMILY.

The Lowells are descended from Percival Lowell of Bristol, England, who settled in Newbury, Mass., in 1639. In the ancient

records of the colony the name is written
Lowle. The family has been distinguished
in every generation. Francis Cabot Lowell
(1775–1817) was among the first to perceive
that the wealth of New England was to come
from manufactures, and it was for him that
the city of Lowell was named. John Lowell
(1743–1802), an eminent judge, was the author of the section in the Bill of Rights, by
which slavery was abolished in Massachusetts. John Lowell, Jr. (1799–1836), was
the founder of the Lowell Institute in Boston.
This great public benefaction, which provides
annual courses of free lectures, was established by a bequest of $250,000 in the testa-
tor's will, written by him while on the summit
of the great pyramid. He was travelling in
the East, and died not long after at Bombay.
Another John Lowell is at present a judge
of the District Court of the United States.
Charles Lowell (1782–1861), a distinguished
divine, was the father of the poet.

The Russells have also an honorable name

in the colony. Richard Russell, from Here-
fordshire, settled at Charlestown in 1640, and
became a prominent man. His son James
bore a manful part in the trying times of
1688–9, and was all his life in positions of
trust.

The Lowells have been men of solid character, earnest, high-minded, philanthropic, and
possessed of strong practical abilities. The
genius for poetry, manifested by the subject
of this sketch and by his brother Robert, was
apparently derived from the maternal line.
Dr. Charles Lowell married Harriet Spence,
a native of Portsmouth, N. H., belonging to
a Scotch family, descended perhaps from Sir
Patrick Spens, celebrated in the old ballad.
A dim tradition to this effect exists, but of
course without the possibility of verification.
The mother of Harriet Spence was named
Traill, a native of one of the Orkneys.[1]

Mrs. Harriet Spence Lowell had a great

[1] The reader remembers Magnus Troil in Scott's novel,
"The Pirate." Troil and Traill are the same.

memory, an extraordinary aptitude for languages, and a passionate fondness for ancient songs and ballads. She had five children : Charles, Robert (the Rev. Robert Traill Spence Lowell, an eminent author and poet), Mary Lowell Putnam, Rebecca, and James Russell, — the subject of our memoir, who was the youngest, born Feb. 22, 1819.

Dr. Lowell was a man of sterling good sense, high principles, strict ideas of duty and honor, and with strongly practical views of life. The children were reared in the plain style that prevailed in New England sixty years ago. They also had their inner senses cultivated by the influence of their mother. They were nurtured with romances and minstrelsy. The old songs were sung over their cradles, and repeated in their early school days, until poetic lore and feeling (foreign grafts in many minds) were as natural to them as the bodily senses. So in right thinking and living, and in study and attainment, they had a noble example in one parent,

while the appreciation of the beautiful came
to them through the other. Mary Lowell
Putnam, born in 1810, is a lady of 'singular mental vigor and of unusual acquire-
ments, and is the author of several important
works. The other daughter, Rebecca, died
in middle age, unmarried. Charles, who died
at Washington about ten years ago, was a
man of superior attainments, and the father
of two brilliant young men, Colonel Charles
Russell Lowell and Lieutenant James Jackson Lowell, both killed in our late civil war.
Mrs. Putnam's only son, Captain William
Lowell Putnam, was killed also in the disas-
trous affair of Ball's Bluff, in the early part
of the war.

BIRTHPLACE AND SURROUNDINGS.

It seldom happens in this country that a
lifetime passes without change of residence;
but, except during his visits abroad, the poet
has always lived in the house in which he
was born.

Elmwood, though not very ancient, has an interesting history. The house was built by Peter Oliver, who was stamp distributer just before the outbreak of the Revolution. It will be remembered that, being waited upon by a Boston committee "of about four thousand," and requested to resign his obnoxious office, Oliver hurriedly complied, and shortly after left the country. The house was next occupied by Elbridge Gerry, an eminent man in his day, from whose crooked plan of districting, the political term "gerrymandering" was derived. After his death it became the property of Dr. Lowell, about a year before the birth of the poet. It is of wood, three stories high, and stands on the base line of a triangle, of which the apex reaches nearly to the gate of Mount Auburn Cemetery. The ample grounds have an abundant growth of trees, most of them planted by the prudent Doctor as a screen from the winds. There are a few native elms; but those which give the name to the estate are

English, sturdy as oaks, standing in front of the house. In front, also, are large and beautiful ash trees.

In the deep space at the rear, in the old days, there was perfect seclusion; it used to seem like the stillness of the woods. The slopes of Mount Auburn, beautiful with native growths, and not then covered by fantastic caprices in marble, are separated only by a narrow street. Dwellings were not numerous or near. All around the enclosure a gigantic hedge stands like a jagged silhovette against the sky. This lofty hedge is made up of a great variety of trees; it bristles with points of tufted pines; it is set at mid-height with thrifty and elbowing willows and dense horse-chestnuts; and beneath it is filled in with masses of shrubs. In the area are broad grassy levels, with a few pear and apple trees, and nearer the house are younger pines, elms, firs, clumps of lilacs, syringas, fleurs-de-lis, gorgeous rugs of striped grass, and other ornamental growths, disdained by modern gardeners, but immortal in the calendars of poets.

Elmwood is full of birds, — robins and their homelier cousins, the brown thrushes, swallows, blue-birds, flaming orioles, yellow-birds, wrens, and sparrows. The leafy coverts are inviolate, and some of the tenants, even the migratory robins, keep house the year round. All are perfectly at home, and they appear to sing all day. On summer evenings, after the chatter of the sparrows has ceased and the robins have sung for curfew, you may hear the *pée-ad* of night-hawks, and the hoarse voices of herons and other aquatic birds, as they fly over from Fresh Pond or the neighboring marshes.

During the lifetime of his father the poet occupied as a study the south front room in the upper story.

Many years have passed since that period, and many changes have occurred in the landscape (and in the beholder!). Perhaps the description which follows may be far from true to-day. Hills have been dug down, and their gravelly sides left bare. Straggling groups of houses have here and there crept out on the wet marsh. The horse-cars have frightened away most of the birds, and almost put to flight the poetical associations. But still faithful memory recalls the prospect, and in her tablets it shines now as it did so long ago. In those treasured pictures we see the distant view from the study windows in their varying aspects. The view is broad and panoramic, comprising portions of Brighton, Brookline, and Roxbury, and ending on the left with the dome of the State House in Boston. The nearer view, over the neighboring lawns, includes the Charles and the marshes. The sluggish river winds through tracts of salt meadow, now approaching camps of meditative willows, now creeping under "caterpillar bridges," and now turning away from terraced villas and turfy promontories. In summer the long coils of silver are set in a ground of green that is vivid and tremulous like watered silk; in autumn the grasses are richly mottled purple, sage, and brown; and the play of sunlight and shadow, while the winds are brushing the velvet this way and that, gives an inimitable life to the picture.

The study contained about a thousand volumes of books, a few classic engravings, water-color paintings by Stillman, Roman photographs, a table with papers and letters in confusion, and a choice collection of pipes. Over the mantel was a panel, venerable and smoky, that had been brought from the house of one of the ancient Lowells in New-bury, on which was painted a group of clergymen in their robes, wigs, and bands, seated about a table, each enjoying a long clay pipe. On an arch above an alcove was this legend in Latin: "In essentials, unity; in non-essentials, liberty; in all things, charity."

This picture, though scarcely a work of art, is interesting for the light it throws upon

the social customs of the clergy of the last
century.

This room was for many years the delightful resort of a few friends, especially on
Sunday afternoons.

After the death of Dr. Lowell, the libraries
were brought together in two connected
rooms on the lower floor. The new study
was more spacious and convenient; but the
precious and undying associations, and the
beautiful outlook, belonged to the upper
chamber.

The house throughout is an example of the
picturesque. In the hall are ancestral portraits (one bearing the date of 1582); busts
of Dr. Charles Lowell and his father; a
stately Dutch clock; and Page's Titianesque
portraits of the poet and his wife in their
youthful days. The prevailing tone of the
rooms is sombre, but the furniture is antique
and solid, such as would make a covetous
virtuoso unhappy for life. Books are everywhere, mostly well chosen standard works in

various languages, including a liberal proportion of plays and romances.

EDUCATION.

The nearest neighbor to Elmwood in 1825
was William Wells, who kept a boys' school,
and from him the poet got most of his early
education. He was for a time, however, pupil
of Mr. Daniel G. Ingraham, who had a highly
successful classical school in Boston. Mr.
Wells was a thoroughly educated English-
man, who had been a member of a publishing house in Boston, — Wells & Lilly. They
published excellent books ; among them, well
edited Latin classics. At that time, when
Lieut.-governor Armstrong was making his
fortune out of the " Life of Harriet Newell "
and " Scott's Family Bible," the Wells &
Lilly classics were neglected, and were sold
for trunk linings. The disheartened pub-
lisher went to Cambridge to diffuse classical
learning in a humbler way. Many distin-

guished men were indebted to Mr. Wells for
their early training. He was a teacher of
the old school, — erudite, formal, and severe;
and it is said that the use of the cane, upon
refractory or idle pupils, was not then one of
the lost arts.

Mr. Lowell entered Harvard College in
his sixteenth year, and was graduated in
1838. Among his classmates and friends
were Charles Devens, a general in our late
war, afterwards a judge of the Supreme
Court of Massachusetts, and lately the Attor-
ney General of the United States; the Rev.
Rufus Ellis; the late Professor Nathan Hale;
the Hon. George B. Loring, M. C.; William
W. Story, the sculptor and poet; Professor
H. L. Eustis; the Rev. J. I. T. Coolidge;
Professor W. P. Atkinson; and others less
known to fame. The Rev. E. E. Hale was
in the class following.

His rank in scholarship was not a matter
of pride. He has been used to say that he
read almost everything, — *except* the text-

books prescribed by the faculty. To certain
branches of study, especially to mathematics,
he had an invincible repugnance. His wide
and multifarious reading was the efficient
fertilization of his mind. Learning, in its
higher sense, came later. The voyages,
travels, romances, poems, and plays he de-
voured were a better aliment for a poet than
the regulation diet of Harvard. His was
a nurture such as Cervantes, Spenser, and
Shakespeare received. Though eminent and
able in many ways, Lowell remains absolutely a poet in feeling. His native genius
was fostered by the associations of a singularly beautiful home; it was nourished by
the works of the dramatists, — masters of
emotion and expression, — by the ideal pictures of poets and novelists, and by the
tender solemnity of the discourses of his
father and of Channing, and others of his
father's friends. Nature and the early sur-
roundings had been alike favorable; and
though he was not a rhyming prodigy like

Pope, lisping in numbers, his first effusions as he came to manhood were in poetic form.

After leaving College, Lowell entered the Law School, and having finished the prescribed course, took his degree of LL.B. in 1840. He opened an office in Boston, but it does not appear that he ever seriously engaged in the practice of law. It is true he wrote a story for the "Boston Miscellany" entitled "My First Client," but that may have been a mythical person. The Rev. Mr. Hale says that his brilliant future was prefigured in his youth, — that his original genius was evident from the first.

HIS FIRST BOOK.

A little before his twenty-second birthday he published a small volume of poems, entitled "A Year's Life." The motto was from Schiller: *Ich habe gelebt und geliebet;* concerning which it may be said that most young men appear to have reached the maturity of

having " lived and loved " at a comparatively
early period. The poems are naturally upon
the subject that inspires youths of one-and-
twenty; and though they do not, many of
them, appear in the author's " complete" collection, they are by no means unworthy of
consideration. They bear a favorable com-
parison with the " Hours of Idleness" and
other first-fruits of genius. The reader is referred to " Irené," " With a Pressed Flower,"
and " The Beggar." The unnamed lady
who is celebrated in the poet's verse, and
who afterwards became his wife, was Miss
Maria White, a person of delicate and spiritual beauty, refined in taste, sympathetic in
nature, and the author of several exquisite
poems. Although most of the pieces in " A
Year's Life " have been set aside by the
severer judgment of the poet, the student
will discover in them many intimations of
the genius that shone out more clearly in
later days. But contemporaries seldom have
the interpretation which comes later with full-

blown success. Margaret Fuller, in "The
Dial," wrote disparagingly of the verses, say-
ing that neither their imagery nor their music
was the author's own.

HE BECOMES AN EDITOR.

In the landscape of letters, dead magazines
are the ruins, often more pathetic than picturesque. Many a young author has felt a
shock at the downfall of his castle, and fortunate is he who is not crushed under it. In
January, 1843, appeared the first number of
the "Pioneer," a magazine of moderate size,
handsomely printed, and illustrated, after the
fashion of the time, with steel engravings.
"J. R. Lowell and Robert Carter" were
announced as "Editors and Proprietors."
Three numbers only were issued before the
publishers failed. The magazine was too
purely literary to be successful. The numbers are now exceedingly scarce, and would
bring an almost fabulous price. Imagine a
magazine with articles by Byron, Shelley,

Coleridge, De Quincey, and Vathek-Beckford! In these three numbers are two of Hawthorne's incomparable stories, "The Birthmark" and "The Hall of Fantasy;" essays upon Beethoven, by John S. Dwight; able articles by John Neal; an Oriental tale by Carter; and articles by Lowell on old plays, and the song writers. But the wealth of the magazine was in its poetry; so many famous people were never enlisted in any one enterprise before or since. Besides the numerous and beautiful contributions of the editor, there were poems by Miss E. B. Barrett (afterwards Mrs. Browning), Edgar A. Poe, Whittier, W. W. Story, T. W. Parsons (a name that is to endure), Jones Very (daintiest of sonneteers), and George S. Burleigh. Poe's poems were "The Telltale Heart" and the well-known "Lenore." Whittier's was entitled "Lines Written in the Book of a Friend:" —

> " On page of thine I cannot trace
> The cold and heartless commonplace,
> A statue's fixed and marble grace," etc.

Parsons contributed poems upon "The Hudson River," "The Shadow of the Obelisk," and "The Tower of Pisa." Story was like Mercutio, a loyal and brilliant second, writing both in prose and verse, and furnishing designs for the engraver.

On the whole, the "Pioneer" was a remarkable periodical, and its only fault was that it was far above the comprehension of the general public of forty years ago.

Before this, Lowell had written some very striking literary essays for the "Boston Miscellany," conducted by his classmate and intimate friend, Nathan Hale.

A SECOND VOLUME OF POEMS.

About three years after the publication of "A Year's Life" appeared another volume of poems well known to readers of to-day. "The Legend of Brittany" and "Prometheus" are the longest; but the most popular are "Rhoecus," "The Shepherd of King Admetus," "To Perdita Singing," "The Forlorn," "The Heritage," "A Parable," etc.

The matter and the manner of this volume were new and not wholly pleasing to the American public of 1844. As we look back and consider the taste of that public, we cannot indulge in any great pride. There were undoubtedly literary circles in each of the principal cities, in which authors and works were estimated with conscientious care; but the general tone was low. The Tityrus of the herds, as Lowell afterwards styled him, was Doctor Griswold. An hour's study of his volumes is better than a sermon on the vanity of human wishes, or a lament over the perishable nature of literary fame.

There were a few names held in honor then that are still more honored now. Longfellow was in the first flush of well-won fame: men had begun to name him in the same breath with Bryant, the recognized chief of the bards. Willis was the Count D'Orsay of letters, the *arbiter elegantiarum*. Holmes was thought to be a bright and witty young man of considerable promise. Whittier was talked of, but people said he was prostituting his muse in the service of fanatics. His lyrics, they thought, had some fire, but an abolition-ist, of course, could not be a poet. The re-tributive tar-kettle would befit him rather than the exhilarating tripod. The first genius of our time — at least among romancers — was absolutely unknown. The "Twice-Told Tales" had been published (1837, 1842), and scarcely a thousand copies had been sold. Pierpont's odes were shouted by schoolboys, and the din of the rhymes on Public Satur-days was like the riveting of steam-boilers. Poe's "Raven" was just about making its sequacious and tantalizing lament. Halleck was the American Campbell. John Neal and Richard H. Dana were great poets, and were sure — some day — to produce something worthy of their fame. "Woodman, Spare that Tree!" "The Old Oaken Bucket," and "Home, Sweet Home," had filled the cup of

national glory full. Mrs. Sigourney, Mrs.
Hale, Miss Gould, and Mrs. Welby were
quoted with Mrs. Barbauld and Mrs. Hemans.
Editors then seemed perched on loftier
heights than now. The Philadelphia magazines, in particular, were thought to be wonderful works of genius and art. Those
magazines in which music strove with milli-
nery, and poetry was entangled with worsted
patterns, and whose plates were fine enough
for perfumery labels, represented a power and
influence with the ingenuous youths of 1844,
which the sober "Atlantic" and the versatile
"Harper" have never since wielded. Poems
admitted into those elegant repositories of the
arts were already classic. To be sure, the
admiring reader at times had some qualms;
as when, for instance, he learned that a spring
gushed "like a fountain of soda," and then
saw that the hard-pressed poet was forced to
lug in "Godey" for a rhyme. But then, this
might be playful.

The revolution in letters has scarcely be-

gun. Pope was still greater than Homer;
Byron was grander than Milton's Satan;
Scott was the only romancer of the ages;
Wordsworth was a dull proser, who took a
pedler for his hero and an idiot for the subject of his pathos. Tennyson was an airy
and effeminate stripling, who had a pleasing
trick of rhyme, and who was properly casti-
gated by Bulwer as

"Out-babying Wordsworth and out-glittering Keats."

In Lowell's verse there was something of
Wordsworth's simplicity, something of Tennyson's sweetness and musical flow, and something more of the manly earnestness of the
Elizabethan poets; but the resemblances were
external; the individuality of the poet was
clear. The obvious characteristic of the
poems is their high religious spirit. It is
not a mild and passive morality that we perceive, but the aggressive force of primitive
Christianity. The vivid conception of the
law of love and of the duties of brotherhood

reminds us of the time when such thoughts were new and startling, and before their vital power had been lost in chanted creeds and iterated forms.

There are several of the poems in this collection which now seem prophetic. They were bold utterances at the time, and were doubtless considered as the rhapsodies of a harmless enthusiast. The ode beginning —

> "In the old days of awe and keen-eyed wonder
> The poet's song with blood-warm truth was rife,"

may be regarded in one aspect as a confession of faith. In force of thought and depth of feeling, and in the energy of its rhythmic movement, it is a remarkable production, whether for a poet of twenty-five or older. Perhaps it is more rhetorical in its energy than maturer taste would approve. It is so compact that a summary is impossible; but it announces in sonorous strains that the mission of the poet, like that of God's prophets, is to attack wrong and oppression, to raise up the weak and reclaim the erring, and to

bring heaven to men.   He decries the bards
who seek merely to amuse, and deplores their
indifference to human welfare.

> " Proprieties our silken bards environ:
>   He who would be the tongue of this wide land
> Must string his harp with chords of sturdy iron,
>   And strike it with a toil-embrownèd hand."

This stirring ode was a fit prelude to the
part our poet was to perform.   If there were
any doubt as to the application, the grand
sonnet to Wendell Phillips, in the same volume, gives it emphasis.

THE ANTI-SLAVERY REVOLUTION.

There are poets whose verse has no re-
lation to time.   "Drink to me only with
thine eyes" might have been sung by any
lyrist from Anacreon to Algernon Swinburne.   Others, like Dante, Milton, Marvell,
and Dryden, who live in times when strong
tides of feeling are surging to and fro, — when
vital principles are in controversy, and the

fate of a people hangs upon the sharp deci-
sion of the hour, — find themselves, whether
they would or no, in the place of actors, — at
once causes and products of the turmoil in
which they are born.

Probably there were never greater changes
in the ideas, habits, and welfare of any civil-
ized people in any half century than were
brought about in the Northern States during
the fifty years from the date of the poet's
birth. This may appear to be an unnec-
essarily strong statement, but it will bear
scrutiny. That half-century witnessed the
astounding changes which followed the application of steam, electricity, and the arts
to practical affairs. In the same period the
bulk of our literature was produced ; and the
press, too, became a power before unknown
in this or any country. Legislation and juris-
prudence were lifted into the light of morals.
Organized benevolence, taking upon itself
the burdens of society, began to make the
Golden Rule an active principle in human

affairs. In fifty years, the United States had outrun the usual progress of centuries.

Europe, too, witnessed great changes in the same period, but they chiefly related to material things. England and France had literatures, arts, societies, and traditions. The United States, as a nation, had none.

Somewhere in our account of the author we should glance at his intellectual lineage, and trace his relations to the thinkers and thoughts of his age.

A LITERARY RETROSPECT.

It is sometimes said of a neglected genius that he is born out of time. But this can never be. As the fauna of any epoch find the fit conditions of sustenance, so the intellectual conditions of any period are the ones appointed for the growth of mind in that time. As the poet embodies in his verse, not only his love of nature and religious feeling, but also the results of philosophy and art, he must be considered in connection with the dominant ideas of his time. The English, who say we have no poetry, are disappointed, probably, in not finding some flavor of strangeness, like that of a wild duck, or some daring novelty of form, as in the prophecies of Walt Whitman; forgetting that for the most part we are still British, though under new conditions, and that, with our heritage and traditions, there could be expected from New World singers only slight variations from ancestral strains. Our colonists represented a high average of English ability and cultivation. Their history shows their blood to have been of the best. Yet in the wilderness literary art languished, and taste was perverted. There was no poetry on the manifest of the "Mayflower" or of the "Arbella;" it had been left behind with England's larks and daisies. A century passed before the savage forests had lost their terrors and the homes of the settlers began to bloom in beauty. Neither prose nor verse flourished until after the revolutionary war.

Our recognized literature began with Bryant and Irving; but its real sources were in Channing, his associates and disciples, or rather in the intellectual movement that followed the decline of ecclesiastical rule.

Channing, so far as he was a conscious agent, was a mild-tempered agitator, remarkable for nobility of character and for a spirituality that was almost angelic. The revolution he led was against the dominant theology, but the influence was felt by millions who never accepted the new doctrines. Clerical limitations became obsolete. People rediscovered Shakespeare, as amateur astronomers discover Jupiter; for the works of the chief of poets had before this been unknown to Puritan libraries. It was found that there were writers and thinkers who were not wearers of Geneva bands. Channing himself was no longer shut up in a remote corner, but was welcomed into the fraternity

of lettered men. Until his essays on Milton,
Fénelon, and Napoleon appeared, European
scholars had never thought of America except in connection with savages, fish, furs,
and rebellion. The breadth and force of
this movement can scarcely be overesti-
mated. Excepting Irving, Cooper, and Poe,
there has not been an American author of
high rank in this century whose intellectual
lineage is not traceable, directly or indirectly,
to Channing and Emerson.

A new light emanated from Nature; or
rather the hills, rivers, and lakes were seen
with anointed eyes. Religion, as well as
literature, was secularized, though the spirit
of Christianity was still supreme. In the
course of time, Christianity got new applica-
tions, and later, democracy had new and
startling definitions. The contest had begun, which in due time was to wash out the
color line with blood. Story and poem,
history and essay, national in tone and
with vital characteristics, gave new life to

society and new lustre to the American
name.

It was in the springtime of the new
thought that our poet was born.

THE ANTI-SLAVERY REVOLUTION MOVES ON.

The function of the critic, as Mr. Stedman
has pointed out, is to anticipate the solid and
dispassionate judgment of posterity upon the
works of to-day, — a task sufficiently difficult, for the critic himself may be enslaved
by the literary fashions which he ought to
resist and deplore. No one can say what
may be the standard of taste a century
hence; for it cannot be known what direction it will receive from some unborn master-
spirit, who will dominate his age. But in
regard to the fundamental laws of ethics
there cannot be any retrogressive movement.
So much is sure.

And to a man in the twentieth century,
looking back, what will appear the great fact

of our time? Indubitably the fulfilment
of the democratic idea in the abolition of
African slavery. It is the most important
event since the discovery of America. The
schemes of Bismarck, Gortschakoff, and Bea-
consfield, or even the gigantic crimes of
Napoleon, are mere games of chess in com-
parison. Yet the time has been when such
an opinion would not have been tolerated in
polite society. The evil was intrenched in
law, defended by statesmen and political
economists, apologized for by clergymen,
and made respectable by custom. Like its
kindred oppressions, absolutism and caste,
(for which we trust Fate has an end at once
effectual and peaceful), slavery was adorned
by the fictile graces of romance and the false
glamour of poesy. The anti-slavery movement has been lately classed with *isms* by
those who see no deeper than the surface
of things, as if it were a fashion, like that
of bran bread; but it was such an *ism* as
Christianity, or Democracy, or International
Peace, or Human Brotherhood.

The position of Lowell was fixed from the beginning. The teachings of Channing and of his father, the doctrines of the New Testament, and the example of his grandfather (author of the liberty clause in our Bill of Rights), all pointed in one direction. He became an abolitionist when the name signified a fanatic and fool. He did not, however, continue long with the theorists who believed the road to universal freedom must be laid over the ruins of the Constitution, but joined with those who meant to extirpate the evil by legal means.

The sincerity and the unflinching zeal of the anti-slavery leaders are not to be questioned, but in the nature of things they were scarcely entertaining. Their discourses were seldom enlivened by wit or humor. It was an awful "burden" they bore. One would as soon expect a joke from Jeremiah. Of literal sarcasm and downright blows there were plenty. It is noticeable, also, that in the first two volumes of Lowell's poems there is

not a single witticism, nor a hint of the comic
power that was to place him among the first
of humorists and satirists. In his "Conversations on the Poets," now out of print and
scarce, there are many keen strokes and ludicrous comparisons, like those in later books
with which the public has become familiar.
In the "Conversations" we see more of the
natural man ; in the early poems we see the
decorous bard in the proprieties of cere-
monial robes. One might believe that the
brilliant raillery which Lowell afterwards
turned upon the supporters of slavery had
its origin in a reaction from the monotonous
oratory of some of his associates. The public, which could bear a great deal of argument upon the national sin, unmoved, was
found to be keenly sensitive to the corus-
cations of wit, and sorely vulnerable to the
arrows of ridicule.

In the summer of 1846, the Mexican war
was in progress, and the abolitionists were
urging (what is now accepted as the truth of

history) that it was waged to obtain new
territory for the extension of slavery, and
thereby to counterbalance the growing power
of the Northern States. President Polk had
been elected to carry out the scheme. The
appeal was to Congress, through the conscience of the nation, to stop the supplies.

HOSEA BIGLOW.

Mr. Lowell wrote a letter in June to the
"Boston Courier," purporting to come from
Ezekiel Biglow, enclosing a poem in the
Yankee dialect, written by his son Hosea,
in which the efforts to raise volunteers in
Boston were held up to scorn.

> "Thrash away, you'll hev to rattle
>   On them kittle-drums o' yourn, —
> 'T aint a knowin' kind o' cattle
>   Thet is ketched with mouldy corn."

Society was puzzled. Critics turned the
homely quatrains over with their talons as
kittens do beetles, shook their wise ears, and
doubted. Politicians thought them flat or

vulgar. Reverend gentlemen, who had not been shocked at the auction of "God's images in ebony," considered the poet profane and blasphemous. But the epithets stuck like burrs. The lines were jingling everywhere. For the first time in the history of the movement the laugh was on the side of the reformers. The peculiarities of some of the more eccentric had furnished the wags heretofore with material for abundant gibes. The long curls of Absalom Burleigh, the masculine declamation of Mrs. Abby Kelley Foster, the sledge-hammer action of Henry C. Wright (perhaps the original of Hawthorne's Hollingsworth?), the white woollen garments, patriarchal beard, and other-world looks of Father Lamson, and the pertinacity of the meek lunatic, Abby Folsom, had made every meeting of the New England Anti-Slavery Society as rare a show for the baser sort as a circus or a negro concert. Now the leading men in church and state were stung by pestilent arrows. Great names

were no protection. The unanswerable ar-
guments of Garrison and the magnificent
invectives which Wendell Phillips had hurled
at well-dressed mobs were now supplemented
by the homeliest of proverbial phrases, set to
the airiest, lilting rhythm, adorned with the
choicest and most effective slang, and ting-
ling with the free spirit that had animated
a line of fighting Puritans since the time of
Naseby. The anti-slavery music was in the
air, and everybody had to hear it.

The more cultivated of the abolitionists
were in ecstasies. Some, however, did not
quite understand it. The levity of tone
hardly accorded with the prophetic burdens
they had been used to. When Charles
Sumner saw the first Biglow poem in the
" Courier," he exclaimed to a friend, " This
Yankee poet has the true spirit. He puts
the case admirably. I wish, however, he
could have used good English ! "

Hosea Biglow kept up the warfare, and
each poem was furnished with a preface and

notes by an imaginary Parson Wilbur.
First, a Mexican-war recruit gave his amusing experiences from the field. Then came
" What Mr. Robinson Thinks." This tickled
the public amazingly, and

> " John P.
> Robinson he
> Sez he wunt vote fer Guvener B.,"

was in every one's mouth, like the " What,
never ? " of " Pinafore." Mr. Robinson was
a refined and studious man, unhappily on the
wrong side of a moral question, and was not
a little annoyed by his " bad eminence ; " but
he is preserved in the Biglow amber, like
an ante-Pharaonic fly. There is a ludicrous,
though perhaps mythical story, that he went
abroad, to get out of hearing the sound of his
own name. As soon as he landed at Liverpool, however, and got to his hotel, he heard
a child in an adjoining room idly singing.
He listened. Yes, it was true ; the detested
refrain had got across the ocean. It was

> " John P.
> Robinson he "

that the baby-ruffian was trolling. He sailed to the Mediterranean, and stopped at Malta. While looking at the ruins of the works of the Templars he observed a party of English not far distant, and presently another infantile voice sang

> " But John P.
> Robinson he
> Sez they did n't know everythin' down in Judee."

About this time the late Dr. Palfrey, the historian, then an able and eloquent member of Congress, had refused to vote for Mr. Winthrop, the Whig candidate for speaker. Hosea Biglow gave expression to the party wrath in a burlesque version of a speech supposed to have been delivered at an indignation meeting in State Street. This was the opening: —

> "No ? Hez he ? He haint, though ? Wut ? Voted agin him ?
> Ef the bird of our country could ketch him, she'd skin him ! "

"A Debate in the Sennit, sot to a Nusry Rhyme" followed; then "The Pious Editor's Creed," and a burlesque of General Taylor's letter accepting the nomination for the presidency. The first letter from Birdofredum Sawin, the Mexican volunteer, created great merriment on account of its local hits, especially those relating to Caleb Cushing, the eminent publicist, who was at that time a general in command. Many of the finest touches are lost upon readers of to-day. The second letter of the series is probably the most fluent, adroit, and effective. The writer had been sadly mutilated, ill-treated, and disillusionèd. He had imagined Mexico as a country

" Ware propaty growed up like time, without no cultivation,
  An' gold wuz dug ez taters be among our Yankee nation,
  Ware nateral advantages were pufficly amazin',
  Ware every rock there wuz about with precious stuns wuz
      blazin',
  Ware mill-sites filled the country up ez thick ez you could
      cram 'em
  An' desput rivers run about a beggin' folks to dam 'em."

The temptation to quote is strong, but there must be a limit. Every couplet contains some felicitous absurdity or hard hit. The volunteer finally descants upon his own merits and available qualities, and offers himself as a candidate for President under the *sobriquet* of "The One-eyed Slarterer." In a third letter, the last of the first series, Mr. Sawin withdraws in favor of "Ol' Zack" (General Taylor).

The poems were finally gathered into a volume, which in comic completeness is without a parallel. The "work" begins with "Notices of the Press," which are delightful travesties of the perfunctory style both of "soft-soaping" and of "cutting up." There happening to be a vacant page, the space was filled off-hand by the first sketch of "Zekle's Courtship:" —

> "Zekle crep' up, quite unbeknown,
> An' peeked in thru the winder,
> An' there sot Huldy all alone,
> 'ith no one nigh to hender."

This is the most genuine of our native idyls. It affects one like coming upon a new and quaint blossoming orchid, or hearing Schu-

mann's *Einsame Blume.* Its appearance in
the " Biglow Papers" was purely an acci-
dent; but it had the air of being an extract,
and it was so greatly admired that the poet
afterwards added stanzas from time to time
to fill out the picture. In the original sketch
there were six stanzas; there are now twenty-
four. Some of the added stanzas are fully
as picturesque and striking as those in the
original improvisation. This is the first: —

> " God makes sech nights, all white an' still
> Fur 'z you can look or listen,
> Moonshine an' snow on field an' hill,
> All silence an' all glisten."

Of the progress of Zekle's passion he says: —

> " But long o' her his veins 'ould run
> All crinkly like curled maple,
> The side she breshed felt full o' sun
> Ez a south slope in Ap'il."

Of Huldy's nature : —

> " For she was jes' the quiet kind
> Whose naturs never vary,
> Like streams that keep a summer mind
> Snowhid in Jenooary."

There is a burlesque advertisement in Latin
of one of Mr. Wilbur's projected works preceding the titlepage. The title itself is a
travesty reminding one of the days of black-
letter quartos. The head-line is " MELIBOEUS
HIPPONAX," as much as to say, " This is a
horse-eclogue." A note informs us of the position of Mr. Wilbur in the learned world,
and refers us to some scores of (imaginary)
societies to which he belongs. The Introduction gives some account of the poet, Hosea
Biglow, and quotes specimens of his serious
verse; and it may be said here that these
supposititious fragments are equal to the best
descriptive poetry of our time. The editor
goes on to discuss the Yankee dialect and its
pronunciation, and at length loses himself in
a maze of genealogical notes and queries.

The notes and comments of the grave and
erudite parson are difficult to characterize.
One sees that he is professionally solemn and
pedantic, and often ridiculous in adhering to
obsolete modes of spelling and to old-fash-

ioned ways. In every page there are striking
thoughts, as well as a profusion of imagery
and an affluence of learning; but there is
also a quaint flavor of antiquity, as if the
honey of his periods had been gathered from
the flowers of Jeremy Taylor, Sir Thomas
Browne, and holy George Herbert. Nothing finer or more characteristic is to be found
in any of Lowell's varied and splendid writings.

Look, for example, at the episodical sketch
of the newspaper, — as graphic as the best
of Carlyle's, — or at the picture of the army
recruit, who is enlisted the morning after a
debauch.

In the course of the volume the parson de-
lineates himself, until he becomes a character as real and as charming as the most
enduring creations of English fiction. To
parody one of the poet's own couplets : —

> And " Wilbur " won't go to oblivion quicker
> Than Adams the parson, or Primrose the vicar.

Which of the dear and stately black-robed

visitors of Elmwood sat for this unrivalled
picture it may not be wise to inquire; but
all the lettered folk above fifty, in Boston
and Cambridge, think they have known him.
The creations of genius, like Colonel Newcome and Don Quixote, are entities; while
historical characters, such as George IV. and
Philip II., may be only shadows.

The " Biglow Papers " end appropriately
with a comic glossary and index. It must be
repeated, by way of emphasis, that, from the
first fly-leaf to the colophon, this is the only
complete and perfect piece of grotesque comedy in existence.

In time, historical notes will be needed, as
they are now for Hudibras. That the Yankee
satire is to be enduring, there can be no doubt.
Its total merits greatly outweigh those of
Hudibras; it has far more humor, and more
quotable lines; and it has a great advantage
in its unique concomitants.

CAMBRIDGE FIFTY YEARS AGO.

As the Yankee peculiarities of the "Biglow Papers" are evidently fresh studies, it might appear strange that they could be wrought out by a resident of Cambridge. The visitor to-day sees magnificent college buildings, broad streets filled with carriages and traversed by horse-cars, and comfortable residences that testify to wealth and luxury. There is still space for gardens and trees, and for open squares and trim lawns; but the tone is urban. If Cambridge is in any respect rural, it is not in the least rustic. The primeval Yankee has become scarce everywhere; he is hardly obtainable as a rare specimen; he is a tradition, like the aurochs or the great bustard. He and his bucolic manners and speech are utterly gone. There is not the echo of a *haöw* in any of the pretentious Italian villas, — nor even in the heavy-timbered mansions, like that of Lowell's friend, G. N., dating from 1656. The "W. I. Goods"

4

store, with clusters of farmers' teams in front,
has yielded to the " march of improvement."
Oxen are as strange as camels, and if there
were a milkmaid to be found, her hands would
smell of *mille-fleurs* or *patchouli*. As soon
expect the return of Jacob and Rachel as to
see again the originals of the poet's Zekle and
Huldy.

The old town as it was in Lowell's boyhood is sketched with rare humor and fine
touches in an article by him, published in
" Putnam's Monthly" in 1853, entitled " Cambridge Thirty Years Ago." It is in the form
of a letter addressed to the " Edelmann
Storg ;" namely, to W. W. Story, the sculptor, Lowell's classmate and intimate friend,
whose name a Swiss innkeeper had once so
misread.

This charming essay, brimming with feeling and full of the graces that delight cultivated readers, shows Lowell himself in his
early maturity in the most striking way.
Later essays may be more profound, but

none of them are so full of the sunshine of
the heart. In this masterly picture we see a
country village, silent and rural. There are
old houses around the bare common, "and
old women, capped and spectacled, still
peered through the same windows from
which they had watched Lord Percy's ar-
tillery rumble by to Lexington." One coach
sufficed for the travel to Boston. It was
"Sweet Auburn" then, a beautiful woodland,
and not a great cemetery. The "Old Road"
from the Square led to it, bending past Elmwood. Cambridgeport was then a "huckle-
berry pastur'," having a large settlement of
old-fashioned taverns, with vast barns and
yards, on the eastern verge. "Great, white-
topped wagons, each drawn by double files
of six or eight horses, with its dusty bucket
swinging from the hinder axle, and its grim
bull-dog trotting silent underneath, . . .
brought all the wares and products of the
country to Boston. These filled the inn-
yards, or were ranged side by side under

broad-roofed sheds; and far into the night the
mirth of the lusty drivers clamored from the
red-curtained bar-room, while the single lan-
tern, swaying to and fro in the black cavern
of the stables, made a Rembrandt of the group
of ostlers and horses below."

Commencement was the great day, to
which the Governor came in state, with
military escort. The annual muster of the
militia, which took place sometimes at Cambridge and sometimes in other neighboring
towns, brought together all the boys of the
county to see the various shows and the
hilarious sport called a " Cornwallis."

If you look at the people, you observe strongly marked social distinctions.
The humbler classes toiled, and were not
ashamed of it. They did not ape the manners of the college circle, nor the luxury of
the wealthy.

The provincial tone was evident. You
have only to talk with an old Bostonian
even now to see how it was. The old

leaders of society had a little of the mock
majesty of Béranger's *Roi d'Yvetôt.* But the
main thing was, that, up to 1830, the manners
and speech of ordinary folk were those of
the seventeenth century. The rustic Yankee
was then a fact. In fifty years, by the aid
of steam and electricity, Boston became a
modern city, on equal terms with the Old
World, a centre of itself, and Cambridge was
developed into a highly cultivated suburb.
The rusticity, leisure, humor, and homespun ·
naturalness were gone. The changes of two
hundred years went by in a lifetime.

Recalling old Cambridge by the aid of
Lowell's reminiscences, we see how the ver-
nacular idioms and the humorous peculiarities
of the people are so naturally reproduced in
his comic verse. No poet of a later day
could have evolved such creations, so perfect
in nature and dress, so thoroughly identi-
fied with the antique world. The acquaintance with the primeval Yankee, begun in the
old town, was extended afterwards by visits

to the Adirondacks and to Moosehead Lake;
and though many artists have made striking
and effective sketches of this vanished original, — notably Mrs. Stowe and Mrs. Rose
Terry Cooke, — it is the belief of the writer,
whose boyhood was passed among the most
perfect native specimens of the race, that
Lowell has surpassed all rivals in depicting
him. This opinion is not based upon the
" Biglow Papers " alone. " Fitz Adam's
Story," of which something will be said
hereafter, is the flowering of Yankee humor
and the visible soul of " Down East."

MARRIAGE AND DOMESTIC LIFE.

Mr. Lowell was married, December 26,
1844, to Miss Maria White of Watertown,
near Cambridge. His domestic life at Elmwood, like the "peace that passeth understanding," could be described only in simile.
It was ideally beautiful, and nothing was
wanting to perfect happiness but the sense of

permanence. Mrs. Lowell was a lovely and accomplished woman, but was never very strong, and her ethereal beauty seemed too delicate for the climate of New England. Children were born to them, but all died in infancy, excepting a daughter (now Mrs. Edward Burnett). Friends of the poet, who were admitted to the study in the upper chamber, remember the pairs of baby shoes that hung over a picture-frame. From the shoes out through the southwest window to the resting-place of the dear little feet in Mount Auburn there was but a glance, — a tender, mournful association, full of unavailing grief, but never expressed in words. Poems written in this period show the depth of parental feeling. Readers remember " The Changeling" and " She Came and Went."

> " As a twig trembles, which a bird
>   Lights on to sing, then leaves unbent,
>   So is my memory thrilled and stirred; —
>   I only know she came and went."

Mrs. Lowell was a writer of sweet and

beautiful verse. One of her poems, "The Alpine Sheep," addressed to a sorrowful mother, was suggested by her own bereavement.

"They in the valley's sheltering care
　　Soon crop the meadow's .tender prime,
　And when the sod grows brown and bare
　　The shepherd strives to make them climb

" To airy shelves of pasture green
　　That hang along the mountain's side,
　Where grass and flowers together lean,
　　And down through mist the sunbeams slide.

"But nought can tempt the timid things
　　The steep and rugged paths to try,
　Though sweet the shepherd calls and sings,
　　And seared below the pastures lie,

" Till in his arms their lambs he takes
　　Along the dizzy verge to go:
　Then, heedless of the rifts and breaks,
　　They follow on, o'er rock and snow.

" And in those pastures, lifted fair,
　　More dewy-soft than lowland mead,
　The shepherd drops his tender care,
　　And sheep and lambs together feed."

Mr. and Mrs. Lowell went to Europe in a sailing vessel in the summer of 1851, and spent a year, visiting Switzerland, France, and England, but living for the most part in Italy. They returned in the autumn of 1852. Mrs. Lowell was slowly, almost imperceptibly, declining. Her fine powers were almost spiritualized, and the loveliness of her nature suffered no change by disease.

> "A blissful vision through the night
>   Would all my happy senses sway
> Of the good Shepherd on the height,
>   Or climbing up the starry way,
>
> "Holding our little lamb asleep, —
>   While, like the murmur of the sea,
> Sounded that voice along the deep,
>   Saying, 'Arise and follow me!'"

The end came in October, 1853, when like a breath her soul was exhaled.

Nine years of wedded life had passed, with loss and sorrow, and often clouded with apprehension, but blessed also by the tenderest joys permitted to mortals.

On the day of Mrs. Lowell's death a child was born to Mr. Longfellow, and his poem, "The Two Angels," perhaps as perfect a specimen of his genius as can be cited, will remain forever as a most touching expression of sympathy.

"'T was at thy door, O friend! and not at mine,
   The angel with the amaranthine wreath,
Pausing, descended, and with voice divine
   Whispered a word that had a sound like Death.

"Then fell upon the house a sudden gloom,
   A shadow on those features fair and thin;
And softly, from that hushed and darkened room,
   Two angels issued, where but one went in."

Mrs. Lowell's poems were collected and privately printed in a memorial volume, with a photograph from Page's portrait; but many of them have been widely copied and become a part of our literature.

THE VISION OF SIR LAUNFAL.

After the brilliant success of the "Biglow Papers," it might have been supposed that Lowell would have continued to produce comic verses; but it would seem that he had not been satisfied with his early serious poetry, and was conscious of the power of accomplishing better results. His next important effort was "The Vision of Sir Launfal," a noble poem, full of natural beauty and animated by high Christian feeling. This was composed in a kind of fury, substantially as it now appears, in the space of about forty-eight hours, during which time the poet scarcely ate or slept. It was almost an improvisation, and its effect upon the reader is like that of the outburst of an inspired singer. The effect upon the public was immediate and powerful; the poem needed no herald nor interpreter. In later poems we may observe more highly wrought imagery, more

Dantesque suggestion, and more philosophic
depth; but "Sir Launfal" is still the poem
most admired by general readers, and it is
the one that best shows the poet's fresh and
exuberant feeling, his native piety, and his
glowing sense of beauty. Every summer
the newspapers remind us how "rare" is
"a day in June," and every winter we read
how

> " Down swept the chill wind from the mountain peak,
>   From the snow five thousand summers old."

The preludes of the two movements of the
poem have become typical in the minds of
our generation.

About the same period came "The Present Crisis," an ardent poem, in a high,
prophetic strain, and in strongly sonorous
measure. This has been often quoted by
public-speakers, and many of its lines are
as familiar as the most trenchant of the
Proverbs : —

" By the light of burning heretics[1] Christ's bleeding feet I
    track."

" Truth forever on the scaffold, Wrong forever on the throne."

" Then to side with Truth is noble when we share her wretched
    crust."

" For Humanity sweeps onward : where to-day the martyr
    stands,
  On the morrow crouches Judas with the silver in his hands."

But the whole poem is a Giant's-Cause-
way group of columnar verses. It is a pity
to pry out specimens; they stand better together.

Mention should be made of "Ambrose,"
a beautiful legend, with a lesson of tolera-
tion; of "The Dandelion" and "The Birch
Tree," both charming pictures, and already
hung in the gallery of fame; and of "An
Interview with Miles Standish," a strong
piece of portraiture, with a political moral.
But of the poems of this period, the most
artistic is "Beaver Brook." There is no
finer specimen of an ideal landscape in mod-

---

[1] Observe that Thomas Hughes has not quoted this cor-
rectly, but has printed "martyrs" for "heretics."

ern verse, — a specimen rich enough in its
suggestions to serve as an object-lesson upon
the poetic art. Beaver Brook, whose valley
was a favorite haunt of the poet, is a small
stream in the present limits of the town of
Belmont, a few miles from Elmwood, not
far from Waverley Station. The mill exists
no longer, but one of the foundation walls
makes a frame on one side for the pretty cas-
cade of

"Armfuls of diamond and of pearl,"

that descends into the "valley's cup." Not
far below is a pasture, in which are the
well-known Waverley Oaks, one of the few
groups of aboriginal trees now standing near
the Massachusetts coast. If a bull be permitted, the largest of the oaks is an elm, now
unhappily dying at the roots. This tree has
a straight-out spread of one hundred and
twenty feet, — sixty feet from the giant trunk
each way The oaks are seven or eight in
number, as like as so many stout brothers,
planted on sloping dunes west of the brook.

They have a human, resolute air. Their
great arms look as if ready to "hit out
·from the shoulder." Elms have their graceful ways, willows their pensive attitudes, firs
their loneliness, but the aboriginal oaks ex-
press the strength and the rugged endurance
of nature. The oaks have been often painted,
but there are many ways of looking at them,
all equally charming.

,HE ATTEMPTS SATIRE.

Mr. Lowell's next venture was again in
the field of satire. "A Fable for Critics," —

> "A Glance at a Few of our Literary Progenies
>   (Mrs. Malaprop's word) from the Tub of Diogenes," —

was

> "Set forth in October, the 31st day,
>   In the year '48, G. P. Putnam, Broadway."

As one looks back, — for 1848, though
it seems but yesterday to some of us, was
really a great while ago, — one hardly knows
whether to be more amazed at the audacity

or the brilliancy of this elaborate *jeu d'esprit*.
The preface declares : —

"I began it, intending a Fable, a frail, slender
thing, rhymey-winged, with a sting in his tail."

There was no doubt about the sting in
the minds of those who felt it ; but private
grievances have been forgotten, except perhaps by the friends of a celebrated woman
between whose renown and whose works
there remains an unaccountable discrepancy.
To bring up the representative authors of a
vain and touchy people for censure (using
the word in its broad original meaning) was
an undertaking of some difficulty and deli-
cacy. But when allowance is made for the
humorous and sportive tone of the Fable,
and we get at the real critical opinions,
either singly or in mass, it is surprising to
see how the poet anticipated the taste of
the coming generation, and how sound and
appreciative, according to present standards,
his judgments are. · Naturally there may be

BEAVER BROOK.

See page 61.

undue warmth here and a shade of coolness there, but there is a general equity and candor. And we must remember that, by and by, the honeyed compliments that are exchanged between living writers are to be forgotten, — that poems and histories are to be scrutinized like coins by money-changers, and reckoned at their just value and no more, and that then will begin the havoc with reputations now fortified behind friendly reviews and journals, and fostered by social, political, and religious cliques. Not one in ten of the popular writers of an epoch can hope to be remembered and read by the next; and it will be found hereafter that Lowell's Apollo was perhaps more generous than severe in his comments upon the literary procession.

The Fable is as full of puns as a pudding of plums. The good ones are the best of their kind, strung together like beads, and the bad ones are so "atrocious" as to be quite as amusing. Materials for any number of Hoods exist in it. Verbal sparkles catch

the eyes of youth; but those who see deeper
find vigorous good sense, power of analysis
and illustration, as well as manly indepen-
dence and just national pride, such as few
comic poets possess. The successive pages
seem like a series of portraits, done by an
artist who knows how to seize upon the
strong points of likeness and avoid caricature; and that is to produce living pictures
in the style of the masters.

The reader who has had his volume by
him since that thirty-first of October knows
it by heart; the judgments are established,
and their curious felicity of phrase always
haunts the memory. Emerson, for example,
is the subject of a keen and almost perfect characterization. If the satirist laughs
(as he may), the reader hesitates to join in
the mirth; for he feels the resistless force, and
sees that the gayety is only the myrtle bough
that covers a sword. Similar praise may be
given to the powerful sketch of Theodore
Parker, although that great preacher was

more tender and more profoundly religious
than he appears in Lowell's verse. Alcott,
" calm as a cloud," and the graceful Willis
are happy specimens. To Bryant the satirist
is perhaps scarcely just,— although the cold-
ness of that great poet's passive muse, and
the want of elasticity and sympathy in his
nature, must be acknowledged. There is
more enthusiasm in the picture of

> " Whittier, whose swelling and vehement heart
> Strains the strait-breasted drab of the Quaker apart."

The lyrical fervor of the verses harmonizes
with the conception of the beloved and ven-
erated bard.

Hawthorne is limned with touches so fine
and aerial that one scarcely sees how it is
done; yet the likeness and the style are inimitable. It is a delicate tribute from one of
the first of poets to the most original and
imaginative of romancers. The estimate of
Cooper, if not wholly complimentary, is mag-
nificently wrought. The lines are imbedded
in thought, and resist change and time.

One of the most charming of these (apparently) off-hand descriptions is that of Philothea, Mrs. Lydia Maria Child, the ablest woman in America in her prime. There is an airy lightness in the treatment of this author that has the effect of *wit in action.* The tale of the "marvellous aloe" is a sufficient instance of the genius of the author. Imagine a commonplace writer attempting to fashion such an illusory legend!

For Irving and for Poe perhaps Lowell's Apollo is no more than just; and as for Judd, although his (neglected) "Margaret" is a work of genius, probably our author means to assert what his fame should have been, rather than what it is. Holmes and Longfellow are generously mentioned, and Lowell's own verse comes in for ironical compliment.

The character of "Miranda" has been supposed by some to be intended as a caricature of Margaret Fuller. If this were true, it would be an instance of unusual severity, for the passages in which "Miranda" figures, though among the most amusing, are terribly sarcastic. Such a woman as the Minerva of the Fable, if there were one, might fully deserve the treatment. Miss Fuller never minced her words, and she always scorned the shelter of sex; but, though she had some traits that drew upon her as much censure as compliment, it is not at all probable that "Miranda" was drawn for her, any more than the sketch of the dull and pedantic reviewer was intended for a well-known Harvard professor. "Miranda" is undoubtedly an imaginary female literary bore.

Of the various episodes there is no room to write. Readers will see that the poet was still zealous for human rights, strongly opposed to the horrors of capital punishment, and energetic in upholding the honor of the republic of letters. And all who trace their origin from Pilgrim or Puritan ancestry will feel a new thrill of pride in the glowing apostrophe to Massachusetts with which the poem ends.

The Fable appeared anonymously, but
such a secret could not be kept. When
people had time to think about it, it was
evident that no other American could have
written it. No poem of the kind in the language equals it in the two aspects of vivid
genius and riotous fun. The Fable careers
like an ice-boat. Breezes fill the light sails,
as if toying with them; but the course is like
lightning, and every movement answers to
the touch of the helm.

No British poet has equalled it. Think of
the dirt of the *Dunciad* and the whooping
savagery of the *English Bards and Scotch
Reviewers!* Yet "Fraser's Magazine" considered the Fable as "clever doggerel."

But when the Fable is calmly surveyed,
though we admit the fervid genius that ani-
mates it, and though we are sure that no
other poet could have written it, or ap-
proached it in comic or serious power and
swiftness, still we must see that it carries
along like a flood a considerable burden of

"inconsidered trifles." There is a lack of proportion and of just treatment here and there which might have been remedied by the labor of revision. It seems like an off-hand sketch, with all the brilliant points and some of the defects that characterize first thoughts hurriedly set down.

COLLECTED POEMS. — UNIVERSITY LECTURES.

In 1849 Mr. Lowell's poems were collected in two volumes; the "Biglow Papers," "A Fable for Critics," and "A Year's Life" were not included. In 1853, and for some years afterwards, he was a frequent contributor to "Putnam's Monthly," conducted by George William Curtis and Charles F. Briggs. Some of his finest productions, both in prose and verse, appeared in that brilliant periodical. In the winter of 1854–55 he delivered a course of twelve lectures on English poetry, in the Lowell Institute. The lectures made a deep impression upon cultivated auditors, and full

reports of them were printed in the Boston
" Advertiser." Their success was due to their
intrinsic merits. The popular lecturer is often
led to imitate the vehement action of a stump
orator and the drollery of a comedian by
turns. Mr. Lowell's pronunciation is clear
and precise, and the modulations of his voice
unstudied and agreeable ; but he seldom, if
ever, raised a hand for gesticulation, and his
voice was kept in its natural compass. He
read like one who had something of importance to utter, and the just emphasis was felt
in the penetrating tone. There were no
oratorical climaxes, and no pitfalls set for
applause. But the weighty thoughts, the earnest feeling, and the brilliant poetical images
gave to every discourse an indescribable
charm. The younger portion of the audience, especially, enjoyed a feast for which
all the study of their lives had been a preparation.

It is probable that by this time our poet
had begun to think of some connection with

the University. The illustrious professor of *belles lettres*, it was known, desired to retire from the chair, and public opinion pointed to Lowell as a proper person for his successor. In the summer of 1854 Mr. Longfellow resigned, and Mr. Lowell was appointed in his place, with leave of absence for two years. He went to Europe to pursue his studies, and remained abroad, chiefly in Dresden, until the spring of 1857, when he returned and began his courses of lectures. No professor was ever more popular with his classes. Students speak of him always in terms of admiration and love. His lectures upon Dante, Chaucer, Shakespeare, and Cervantes, in particular, have made an ineffaceable impression upon the scholars of Harvard.

In the two years of residence abroad, he had time for much methodical reading, particularly in the literatures of modern Europe; but, in truth, the studies which made him a distinguished scholar had been begun long before, and have been pursued ever since.

His power of assimilation has been even more remarkable than his facility of acquisition. The best things in all tongues naturally gravitated to him; and it was difficult for any but the most curiously learned to say whether he seemed more at home with the philosophic authors of Germany, the great poet of Italy, the immortal romancer of Spain, the brilliant wit and classic finish of the French, or with the long line of poets, chroniclers, and thinkers of our old home. His resources were ample for almost any undertaking. His characteristics as a writer of prose will be considered in the proper place; but it may be observed here that, along with his varied studies, he had early cultivated, unconsciously perhaps, a learned, rich, and allusive style, — singularly apt and forcible, and teeming with poetic illustrations.

CONVERSATIONS ON THE POETS.

The germs of his literary criticism are
to be found in his "Conversations on the
Poets," published in his twenty-fifth year.
The book is a valuable part of his literary
biography. The sentences give an impression of prolixity at first, not so much of words
as of teeming, struggling thought. They at-
test the yet untrained luxuriance of genius.
The doctrines are of the modern school, in
opposition to the formal antithesis and the
superficial glitter of Pope and his French
masters, and in favor of the simplicity
and vigor of the Elizabethan authors, and
of Chaucer. A good part of the volume
is devoted to the modernization of passages from Chaucer, and to comments upon
Spenser, Shakespeare, Chapman, Drayton,
Ford, Marlowe, and other dramatic poets.
Marvell is also a favorite, and Jeremy Taylor is dwelt upon with a poet's enthusiasm.
Of the moderns, he appears to hold Keats

and Tennyson in highest esteem, though the
strength and naturalness of Wordsworth are
admitted. We make room for a few sentences : —

" You may claim for Pope the merit of an envi-
ous eye, which could turn the least scratch upon
the character of a friend into a fester, — of a
nimble and adroit fancy, and of an ear so nig-
gardly that it could afford but one invariable
cæsura to his verse ; but when you call him
poet, you insult the buried majesty of all earth's
noblest and choicest spirits. Nature should lead
a true poet by the hand, and he has far better
things to do than to busy himself in counting the
warts upon it, as Pope did."

" Pope treated the English language as the
image-man has served the bust of Shakespeare
yonder. To rid it of some external soils he has
rubbed it down till there is no muscular expression left."

" A poet could not write the ' Dunciad,' nor
read it."

The citations are given for the opinions,
not as specimens of the style.

From the time of the Conversations (1845) to that of the first lectures (1855) there was a marked change, but only the change from adolescence to manhood. It was the normal development of an active, original, and poetic mind. Even the matter of the lectures underwent a change before being presented to the public, fifteen years later. Only a small part of the critical labors has been printed, but the most important subjects have been elaborated into the stately essays which form the last three volumes of prose.

FIRESIDE TRAVELS.

The volume of "Fireside Travels," containing the sketch of old Cambridge already mentioned, was published in 1864. The articles were written when Lowell was thirty-four, a mature young man, chastened and thoughtful, but still joyously young. It was the period when fresh feeling was in the ascendant, and when the poet had no inclination to exchange the creative pencil for the scalpel of the critic. There is a tide in the soul of man, and it comes neither too early nor too late in life, — a time when the poet or artist is at his best, — hand and brain and heart at one. The youth conceives, but often fails adequately to embody the creation. The veteran would gladly fulfil his soul's behest, but the feeling has gone with the visions of his morning. The enthusiasm and creative power belong to young blood. What the ardent youth achieves may lack the maturer graces, but it will be in his springtime, if ever, that he will put his ideas of beauty into enduring forms.

"Fireside Travels," among prose works, is the product of Lowell's best days. It is exuberant, but not in the least crude. In fact, the art is quite as remarkable as the fertility. Pages appear like the soil of hot-house beds, with thoughts, serious, jocose, learned, allusive, sprouting everywhere. It does not matter where the reader opens, for every sentence has some salient or recondite charm. The Italian journals, the life in the Maine woods, and the reminiscences of Cambridge are equally fascinating. As mere studies of a highly ornamented style they are perfect. It is true that in graver essays Lowell has displayed more profundity, more learning, and more grand figures; but those who know the earlier volume well will surely turn to it oftener. The sketches of President Kirkland, Professors Popkin and Sales, and of Allston the painter, and others, — all too brief, — are not only delightful in style, but are full of warm and generous feeling that knits author and reader henceforth in an indissoluble bond. One often wonders, after reading of the Cambridge dons for the twentieth time, where there is to be found another essay like it. In Thackeray's essays there are points of resemblance. The "Roundabout Papers," "The Four Georges," and the "English Humorists," though totally different in matter and in style, give a similar

inward satisfaction. A comfortable feeling
remains long after the verbal felicities have
been enjoyed and passed out of remembrance.

HIS SECOND MARRIAGE.—THE "ATLANTIC."

Two important events in his life occurred
in 1857. Mr. Lowell was married in Septem-
ber to Miss Frances Dunlap, of Portland,
Maine, who had had charge of the education
of his only daughter during his residence
abroad. For a time he resided in Oxford
Street, Cambridge, with Dr. Estes Howe,
who had married a sister of Maria White
Lowell; but not long after he returned to
Elmwood.

In November, "The Atlantic Monthly"
was started under the auspices of the chief
authors of New England, with Mr. Lowell as
editor-in-chief. One purpose of the magazine was to give the active support of letters
to the anti-slavery cause, and in this respect
its position was decided. Before this there

was no popular magazine with positive opinions. The editor's contributions were both in prose and verse, and were conspicuous for their force, and often for their pungent wit. At the beginning, the political articles were written by an eminent author of New York, but after a time the department was managed by the editor alone.

In less than two years from the time the "Atlantic" was started, both the senior members of the publishing house, Messrs. Phillips, Sampson, & Co., died, and the magazine passed into the hands of Messrs. Ticknor & Fields. Mr. Lowell continued as editor until 1862, when he was succeeded by Mr. Fields.

In the first three volumes there are a few notable articles from Lowell, including two of a political character, entitled "A Pocket Celebration of the Fourth," and "A Sample of Consistency." Among the poems may be mentioned "The Dead House," — one that no reader ever forgets. It appears to have haunted the memory of some poets also.

"The Origin of Didactic Poetry," in the first
number, is an amusing fable, in the poet's
happiest vein. Several fine poems appeared
in the first volume, among them "The Nest,"
which does not appear in the "complete"
collection.

As Lowell was never given to the production of merely fanciful verses, — the very
lightest of his thistledowns having some seed
in them, — and as his mind always moved to
the tides in the ocean of human thought and
feeling, it will not appear strange that the
great events following the election of President Lincoln gave a new direction to his active faculties. In feeling, as before observed,
he is primarily a poet; but he is also, like
Milton, a thinker, with a fund of uncommon
practical sense, and as much of a man of
action as any retired scholar can be. The
topsails may fill or flutter in celestial airs
while the hull struggles in the heaving sea.

In earlier days there were dreams of the
peaceful solution of all controversies; swords

were to be beaten into ploughshares; kings
and nobles were to be submerged in the ris-
ing tide of humanity. "Round the earth's
electric circle" went the flash of sympathy.
The young Victor Hugos of Heidelberg and
Jena, Paris and Bologna, Berlin and London,
were in accord. Conservatism was frightened: the millennium was coming; the doctrines of American democracy were to have
a generous, practical illustration in the gov-
ernments of enlightened nations. Literature
was animated by a high philanthropic spirit.

The poetry of the new school was as pure
as the Gospels, and as uncompromising as the
early church. Brook Farm, with its æsthetic
communism, had been one of the signs of the
times, — a precursor, it was hoped, of Arca-
dian days to come. Plainness in dress prevailed, even among the rich and delicately
bred. Lowell's youthful portrait, by Page,
represents him in a coarse brown coat, with
his broad shirt-collar turned down, and with
long hair, parted at the centre of the forehead,

and hanging in careless grace upon ruddy and wind-tanned cheeks. The poetry of the picture is in the calm and dreamy eyes, looking out of a shadow of bronze mist.

But the time of boundless hope for humanity went by, and after the reaction the conservatives were stronger than ever before. In this country the passage of the Fugitive Slave Bill was the answer to the efforts of the abolitionists. When the contest between North and South was settled, as far as ballots could do it, by the election of Lincoln, the struggle was immediately transferred to the field, and for four years the power and endurance of the two sections were tried to the uttermost. The rebellion surprised most people, but wise observers had long seen its approaching shadow. A Massachusetts governor procured military overcoats months before the rattle of drums was heard.

HOSEA BIGLOW AGAIN.

The " Atlantic " had a number of vigorous political articles in prose, and, a few months after the outbreak, Lowell again set up the simple Biglow stage with the old *dramatis personæ* to ridicule secession. The first attempt was an epistle in rhyme from the veteran Birdofredum Sawin to Hosea. The hero of the Mexican war had become a Southerner, — had been tarred and feathered (perhaps by way of acclimatization), — had been in the State's Prison on a groundless charge, and on his release had married a widow, the owner of slaves. He had therefore reached an eminence from which he could look down on the "mudsills" of his native State.

"'Nough said, thet, arter lookin' roun', I liked the place so wal,
Where niggers doos a double good, with us atop to stiddy 'em,
By bein' proofs o' prophecy an' suckleatin' medium,
Where a man 's sunthin' coz he 's white, an' whiskey 's cheap
    ez fleas,
An' the financial pollercy jes' sooted my idees,

Thet I friz down right where I wuz, merried the Widder
  Shennon,
(Her thirds wuz part in cotton-land, part in the curse o'
  Canaan,)
An' here I be ez lively ez a chipmunk on a wall,
With nothin' to feel riled about much later 'n Eddam's fall."

The correspondent desires that Hosea
should break the news of his Southern mar-
riage to the wife he had left behind.

" I want thet you should grad'lly break my merriage to Jerusby,
  An' there's a heap of argymunts thet's emple to indooce ye :
  Fust place, State's Prison, — wal, it's true it warn't for
    crime, o' course,
  But then it's jest the same fer her in gittin' a divorce ;
  Nex' place, my State's secedin' out hez leg'lly lef' me free
  To merry any one I please, pervidin' it's a she ;
  Fin'lly, I never wun't come back ; she need n't hev no fear
    on 't,
  But then it's wal to fix things right, fer fear Miss S. should
    hear on 't ;
  Lastly, I've gut religion South, an' Rushy she's a pagan
  Thet sets by th' graven imiges o' the gret Nothun Dagon ;
  .   .   .   .
  An' ef J. wants a stronger pint than them thet I hev stated,
  Wy, she's an aliun in'my now, an' I've been cornfiscated."

The light and mocking tone of this epistle
is in strong contrast with the deep and

almost passionate feeling that breathes in
the later poems of the series. In the summer and autumn of 1861 people thought the
campaign was to be something like a picnic
excursion.

JONATHAN TO JOHN.

The capture of the rebel commissioners,
Mason and Slidell, by Commodore Wilkes,
— a resolute and truly British proceeding, —
though in violation of the law of nations,
will forever endear his name to the American
people. None but lawyers will consider the
persons of those emissaries more sacred than
spies or munitions of war. Still we must
approve the cautious policy, or the magna-
nimity of Lincoln, — whichever it was, — that
decided upon returning the two white ele-
phants. The surrender, however, was a
great trial to pride, particularly in the Eastern States, where the memory of England's
arrogant assumption of sovereignty on the
seas was still rankling. Lowell has, prob-

ably, better than any one, expressed this
mingled feeling in his famous "Yankee
Idyll." The preface by the Rev. Mr. Wilbur shows that gentleman at his best. It
is worth all the starched formality of the
State papers on the subject; for it puts the
case to the British ministry in a way that
leaves its unfriendliness, in recognizing the
rebels as belligerents and in fitting out priva-
teers, without even the rags of hypocrisy to
cover it. In this unaccredited despatch Earl
Russell might read the sentiments of the
indignant Northern people. The style of
the preface is curiously apt. The Latin
quotations are numerous, as usual, and the
pungent phrases have an unstudied air, as
if pugnacity were as natural as breathing.
But under the equable flow of discourse one
feels there is a patriotic fire that burns un-
quenchably.

International law has gained by the controversy. The English ministers were right
and the Commodore was wrong; but Wilkes

is a hero forevermore, and Earl Russell and his associates are accomplices in a national crime.

In the stern Idyl that follows, the talk between Concord Bridge and Bunker Hill Monument sounds like the click between flint and steel. Concord expresses the natural wrath of the nation ; Bunker Hill its calm reason and wise policy. The Bridge calls up old grievances : —

> "*I* recollect how sailors' rights was won,
> Yard locked in yard, hot gun-lip kissin' gun.
>   .   .   .   .
> Better thet all our ships an' all their crews
> Should sink to rot in ocean's dreamless ooze,
>   .   .   .   .
> Than seek sech peace ez only cowards crave :
> Give me the peace of dead men or of brave ! "

Hosea, we see, grows oratorical, but the heart forgives the swelling tone when such a feeling inspires it.

The Bridge keeps a little ahead in the discussion, as anger generally outruns prudence ; and there follows a terrible arraignment of

the English before the tribunal of the nations.
Those who lived as mature men and women
in those times well remember the thrilling
apostrophe with which the poem concludes.
The dialect is unchanged, but it flows with
resistless energy. The poet has transmuted
each rustic phrase into a fiery symbol, and
the images loom up, majestic as the homespun heroes he celebrates.

> "O strange New World, thet yit wast never young,
>   Whose youth from thee by gripin' need was wrung,
>   Brown foundlin' o' the woods, whose baby-bed
>   Was prowled roun' by the Injun's cracklin' tread,
>   An' who grew'st strong thru shifts an' wants an' pains,
>   Nussed by stern men with empires in their brains,
>
>   .   .   .   .
>
>   Thou, skilled by Freedom an' by gret events
>   To pitch new States ez Old-World men pitch tents,
>   Thou, taught by Fate to know Jehovah's plan
>   Thet man's devices can't unmake a man,
>   An' whose free latch-string never was drawed in
>   Against the poorest child of Adam's kin, —
>   The grave 's not dug where traitor hands shall lay
>   In fearful haste thy murdered corse away ! "

Then came the impressive ballad, in which
all the force of the preceding argument was
fused into a passionate deprecation.

" It don't seem hardly right, John,
 When both my hands was full,
To stump me to a fight, John, —
 Your cousin, tu, John Bull !
  Ole Uncle S. sez he, ' I guess
  We know it now,' sez he,
 'The lion's paw is all the law,
  Accordin' to J. B.,
  Thet 's fit for you an' me ! '

. . . . . .

" Shall it be love, or hate, John ?
 It 's you thet 's to decide ;
Ain't *your* bonds held by Fate, John,
 Like all the world 's beside ?
  Ole Uncle S. sez he, ' I guess
  Wise men forgive,' sez he,
 ' But not forget ; an' some time yet
  Thet truth may strike J. B.,
  Ez wal ez you an' me.' "

FAME.

The satires of Hosea Biglow had been
appreciated by anti-slavery men and by
judges of poetic art, — a very select company in any age, — but the ballad " Jona-
than to John," appealing to a natural patriotic
pride, became immediately popular. Party

dissensions were stilled during the awful struggle for national existence, and though England was knit to us by ties of kindred and by a community of letters and laws, there was no one to defend her course in any Northern State. The statement of our country's case against the "mistress of the seas" was received with universal applause.

The author who had patiently waited for recognition could now be satisfied, if fame had been his desire. Many literary reputations have been built up with as much forethought and tact as go to the making of fortunes. Lowell would not be human if he did not relish a good word better than an ill one; but he never asked for the one or deprecated the other. His fame came as slowly as if it had been extorted from an unwilling public, — as if it had been weighed out to him, ounce by ounce, from an inexorable balance. When unjustly criticised, if a friend proposed to take the field, he would say, "Don't bother yourself with any sympathy for me under my supposed sufferings from critics. I don't need it in the least. If a man does anything good, the world always finds it out, sooner or later; and if he does n't, why the world finds *that* out, too, — and ought."

There is a similar consolation in a couplet from the "Fable for Critics:" —

> " All the critics on earth cannot crush with their ban
> One word that 's in tune with the nature of man."

INSIDE VIEW OF SECESSION.

Mr. Sawin was next heard from in a letter to Hosea, detailing his "conversion," descanting upon the superior strain of Southern blood, and anticipating the creation of a batch of nobles as soon as Secession should be established. His new wife, he says, was a Higgs, the "first fem'ly" in that region, —

> " On her Ma's side all Juggernot, on Pa's all Cavileer."

After some ridicule of "Normal" blood and

Huguenot descent, we have an inside view
of Secession, — salt selling by the ounce,
whiskey getting "skurce," and sugar not to
be had. Meantime the corner-stone of the
new State is a powder-cask, and Jeff. Davis
is "cairn the Constitooshun roun' in his hat."
The ironical compliments of Mr. Sawin to
the national Congress conclude the letter.

A burlesque message of Davis to the Con-
federate Congress and a speech of a Southern sympathizer in a secret (Northern) caucus
followed, and then came one of the most
justly celebrated of the series, entitled,
"Sunthin' in the Pastoral Line." One other,
soon to be mentioned, rises to a higher key;
but this Pastoral is the perfection of descriptive poetry. It is wonderful to see how the
dialect is moulded by the thought. When
the sights and sounds and odors of spring
come to mind, the crabbed speech becomes
poetical, as a plain face glows into beauty
on the sudden impulse of the heart. There
have been many serious and comic descrip-

tions of the waywardness and coquetry of
a New England spring, but this may serve
as a *résumé*, like a cyclopædia. Every line
suggests a picture, neither stately nor jocose,
but like nature itself.

There are ancient musical "modes" that
are neither major nor minor, in which the
movement from grave to joyous chords is
made without modulation and without shock.
So in this unique Pastoral we pause over the
loveliest images and hints of tantalizing likeness; and, while the pleasure still lingers, we
find that Hosea has gone on, whittling away at
some problem, and using his mother-wit with
unconscious and aphoristic art. To give instances would be to quote the poem. Sooner
quote any one of the thousand clumps of rosy
mist from Mr. Sargent's acre of azaleas.

HOSEA BECOMES PASTORAL AND IDYLLIC.

After a while, Hosea, declaring himself
"unsoshle as a stone," because his "innard
vane" has been "pintin' east" for weeks

together, starts off to lose himself in the pine woods. He comes to a small deserted "school'us'," a favorite resort when in a bluish revery, and, sitting down, he falls asleep. Here comes a passage that must be quoted : —

> "Our lives in sleep are some like streams thet glide
> 'Twixt flesh an' sperrit boundin' on each side,
> Where both shores' shadders kind o' mix and mingle
> In sunthin' thet ain't jes' like either single;
> An' when you cast off moorin's from To-day,
> An' down towards To-morrer drift away,
> The imiges thet tengle on the stream
> Make a new upside-down'ard world o' dream."

A Pilgrim Father appears.

> "He wore a steeple-hat, tall boots, an' spurs
> With rowels to 'em big ez ches'nut burrs."

This was Hosea's remote ancestor, once a colonel in the parliamentary army. He makes himself known, and tells his descendant that he had

> "worked round at sperrit-rappin' some,
> An' danced the tables till their legs wuz gone,
> In hopes o' larnin' wut wuz goin' on.
> But mejums lie so like all-split
> Thet I concluded it wuz best to quit."

THE MILL-WHEEL.

See page 62.

In his youth, he tells Hosea, he had youth's pride of opinion : —

> "Nothin' from Adam's fall to Huldy's bonnet,
> Thet I warn't full-cocked with my jedgment on it."

He makes a parallel between the cause of the loyal North and that of the Commonwealth against King Charles, and exclaims : —

> "'Slav'ry 's your Charles, the Lord hez gin the exe —'
> 'Our Charles,' sez I, 'hez gut eight million necks.'"

He likens the rebellion to the rattle of the snake, and adds : —

> "It 's Slavery thet 's the fangs an' thinkin' head,
> An', ef you want selvation, cresh it dead!"

PARSON WILBUR.

In the preface to the next poem the death of the Rev. Mr. Wilbur is announced, and, shadow though he be, the reader feels his loss like that of a friend.

The thought of grief for the death of an imaginary person is not quite so absurd as it might appear. One day, while the great

7

novel of "The Newcomes" was in course of publication, Lowell, who was then in London, met Thackeray on the street. The novelist was serious in manner, and his looks and voice told of weariness and affliction. He saw the kindly inquiry in the poet's eyes, and said, "Come in to Evans's, and I 'll tell you all about it. *I have killed the Colonel.*" So they walked in and took a table in a remote corner, and then Thackeray, drawing the fresh sheets of manuscript from his breast pocket, read through that exquisitely touching chapter which records the death of Colonel Newcome. When he came to the final *Adsum*, the tears which had been swelling his lids for some time trickled down upon his face, and the last word was almost an inarticulate sob.

Let us go on with Mr. Wilbur. In the letter which gives the news of his death, the writer declares that the good clergyman's life was shortened by our unhappy civil war.

The train of thought which follows probably represents the state of the poet's own mind. Mr. Wilbur, in an unfinished letter, left behind, says: "It has been my habit, as you know, on every recurrence of this blessed anniversary (Christmas), to read Milton's 'Hymn of the Nativity,' till its sublime harmonies so dilated my soul and quickened its spiritual sense, that I seemed to hear that *other* song which gave assurance to the shepherds that there was One who would lead them also in green pastures and beside the still waters. But to-day I have been unable to think of anything but that mournful text, 'I came not to bring peace, but a sword.'"

The poem sent with the good parson's last letter is a vigorous appeal for ending the war, — a protest against vacillation and half-heartedness. The prelude shows the heart's desire: —

> "Ef I a song or two could make
> Like rockets druv by their own burnin',
> All leap an' light, to leave a wake
> Men's hearts an' faces skyward turnin'!"

The key-note of the poem is in the last couplet of the first stanza: —

> " Wut 's wanted now 's the silent rhyme
>   'Twixt upright Will an' downright Action."

Truly the struggle had been long and
agonizing.

YANKEE HUMOR AND PATHOS.

If the test of poetry be in its power over
hearts, the tenth in this series must be placed
in the highest rank. The beginning is quaint,
simple, and even humorous, but with a sub-
dued tone; there is no intimation of the
coming pathos; nor are we conscious of the
slow steps by which we are led, stanza by
stanza, to the heights where thought and
feeling become one.

Admirers of the great actor, William War-
ren, who is called a comedian, but who is
possessed of the rarest pathetic power, have
often been indignant when rural auditors,
imagining that everything uttered by the

favorite *must* be funny, giggle and clap at the marvellous accents and action which move all thinking people to sudden tears. It is with some kindred apprehension that the present writer ventures to quote a stanza in the native dialect; though full of delicate feeling, expressed with the inimitable art of a great poet, the unlettered style suggests only what is ridiculous "to the general," who can see nothing touching in the sentiment of a rustic, and are not softened by tears unless shed into a broidered handkerchief.

> "Sence I begun to scribble rhyme,
>   I tell ye wut, I hain't ben foolin';
> The parson's books, life, death, an' time
>   Hev took some trouble with my schoolin';
> *Nor th' airth don't git put out with me,*
>   *Thet love her 'z though she wuz a woman;*
> *Why, th' ain't a bird upon the tree*
>   *But half forgives my bein' human.*"

The poet goes on recalling —

> "Sights innercent ez babes on knee,
>   Peaceful ez eyes o' pastur'd cattle;"

The "yaller pines,"

> " When sunshine makes 'em all sweet-scented,
> An' hear among their furry boughs
> The baskin' west-wind purr contented ; "

Then

> " The farm-smokes, sweetes' sight on airth,
> Slow thru the winter air a-shrinkin'
> Seem kin' o' sad, an' roun' the hearth
> Of empty places set me thinkin'."

This brings to mind the poet's slain nephews:

> " Why, hain't I held 'em on my knee ?
> Did n't I love to see 'em growin',
> Three likely lads ez wal could be,
> Hahnsome an' brave an' not tu knowin' ? "
>
> .   .   .   .
>
> " Wut 's words to them whose faith an' truth
> On War's red techstone rang true metal,
> Who ventered life an' love an' youth
> For the gret prize o' death in battle ?
> To him who, deadly hurt, agen
> Flashed on afore the charge's thunder,
> Tippin' with fire the bolt of men
> Thet rived the Rebel line asunder ? "

In this last stanza the direct, weighty words, the intensity of feeling, and the force of the bold images create a sensation that is nothing less than sublime. It refers, as readers perhaps know, to the poet's nephew, General Charles Russell Lowell, at the battle of Winchester, who, though he had received a wound which he knew to be mortal, mounted his horse, and led his troops in a brilliant charge, was again mortally wounded, and shortly after expired.

Here the sorrowing Hosea exclaims : —

> "'T ain't right to hev the young go fust,
> All throbbin' full o' gifts an' graces."

But the lines are palpitant like naked nerves, and every word is like the branch plucked by Dante, which trickled blood. We must leave the poem with its aching burden, and forbear to copy even its noble conclusion.

HOSEA AS AN ORATOR.

The last of the "Biglow Papers" is a speech of Hosea in the March town meeting. The preface is by the Meliboeus-Hipponax himself, and is a delightful *ragout* of Yankee phrases, peppered with pungent wit. His summary or "argymunt" of a popular speech has been often copied, and has done service in many comic readings; but its irresistible drollery keeps it fresh.

Those who know the real sources of current proverbial slang, and of much of the wit of Yankeeland, need not be told that the "Biglow Papers" have furnished enough for the stock in trade of a dozen professional humorists.

" THE ARGYMUNT.

" Interducshin, w'ich may be skipt. Begins by talkin' about himself: thet 's jest natur an' most gin'ally allus pleasin', I b'leeve I 've notist, to *one* of the cumpany, an' thet 's more than wut you can say of most speshes of talkin'. Nex' comes the gittin' the goodwill of the orjunce by lettin' 'em gether from wut you kind of ex'dentally let drop thet they air about East, A one, an' no mistaik, skare 'em up an' take 'em as they rise. Spring interdooced with a fiew approput flours. Speach finally begins witch nobuddy need n't feel oboly-gated to read as I never read 'em an' never shell this one ag'in. Subjick staited; expanded; delayted; extended. Pump lively. Subjick staited ag'in so 's to avide all mistaiks. Ginnle remarks; continooed; kerried on; pushed furder; kind o' gin out. Subjick *re*-staited; dielooted; stirred up permiscoous. Pump ag'in. Gits back to where he sot out. Can't seem to stay thair. Ketches into Mr. Seaward's hair. Breaks loose ag'in an' staits his subjick; stretches it; turns it; folds it; onfolds it; folds it ag'in so 's 't no one can't find it. Argoos with an imedginary bean thet ain't aloud to say nothin' in repleye. Gives him a real good dressin' an' is settysfide he 's rite. Gits into Johnson's hair. No use tryin' to git into his head. Gives it up. Hez to stait his subjick ag'in; doos it back'ards, sideways, eendways, criss-cross, bevellin', noways. Gits finally red on it. Concloods. Concloods more. Reads some xtrax. Sees his subjick a-nosin' round arter him ag'in. Tries to avide it. Wun't du. *Mis*states it. Can't conjectur' no other plawsable way of staytin' on it. Tries pump. No fx. Finely concloods to conclood. Yeels the flore."

In the course of the speech that follows, Mr. Biglow observes: —

> " N. B.   Reporters gin'lly git a hint
>   To make dull orjunces seem 'live in print,
>   An', ez I hev t' report myself, I vum,
>   I 'll put th' applauses where they 'd *ough' to* come!"

Little did the orator of Jaalam suppose that his shrewd plan would be copied years afterwards by a great lecturer.

RECONSTRUCTION.

The speech is supposed to have been made in April, 1866, a year after the surrender of Lee; and the "subjick" is naturally upon what has since been called "reconstruction." In the light of the history of the last dozen years, the sound sense and almost prophetic character of this speech are remarkable. It is free from bitterness, but it states with un-flinching rigor the only conditions of national unity. Of these the chief is

> " the old Amerikin idee,
>   To make a man a Man an' let him be."

The President, Andrew Johnson, comes in for the hardest hits.

" ' Nobody ain't a Union man,' sez he,
'Thout he agrees, thru thick an' thin, with me ;"

. . . .

" Is this ere pop'lar gov'ment thet we run
A kin' o' sulky, made to kerry one ? "

. . . .

" Who cares for the Resolves of '61,
Thet tried to coax an airthquake with a bun ? "

. . . . . .

" He thinks secession never took 'em out,
An' mebby he 's correc', but I misdoubt ;
Ef they war n't out, then why, 'n the name o' sin,
Make all this row 'bout lettin' of 'em in ? "

[Derisive cheers.]

" O, did it seem 'z ef Providunce
Could ever send a second Tyler ?
To see the South all back to once,
Reapin' the spiles o' the Freesiler,
Is cute ez though an ingineer
Should claim th' old iron for his sheer
Coz 't was himself that bust the biler ! "

[Gret laughter.]

THE DECAY OF THE YANKEE DIALECT.

From this comparatively long, but really
brief and inadequate, synopsis the reader
may infer the high aim and definite moral

purpose of the " Biglow Papers," and their
intimate connection with our national history. Poetry seldom needs comment; the
lightning flash explains itself; and, in truth,
comment rarely carries admiration along with
it into the mind of the reader. But the " Biglow Papers " are in a foreign tongue for all
city folk; and even in the country the *patois*
has for a long time been faithfully grubbed
up by school-ma'ams, like the Canada thistle.
An appreciation of Burns comes after as much
study as the Provençal songs require, and it
is only one " native and to the manner born "
who is able to perceive and to convey by
vocal inflections the right effect of the eli-
sions and contractions that make such thorny
thickets of Yankee verse. On the other hand,
few of those who have inherited knowledge
of the dialect have the cultivation and the
innate feeling for the essence of poetry,
which many of Lowell's productions ask of
the reader. Between the difficulties of the
dialect, and the high demands of all true

poetry upon the intelligence, the highest
qualities of the "Biglow Papers" are far
enough removed from popular apprehension.
But whoever will give them such a study as
will insure mastery, will be rewarded by the
knowledge of some of the most vigorous,
impassioned, humorous, dainty, quaint, and
glowing verse of our century.

As, at the beginning, Lowell was mentioned as one of the forces and products of
the age, — an actor and sympathizer in its
moral and political movements, — it has been
deemed essential to dwell more upon the
works which have become a part of our history. The usual topics of poetry — nature
and man — have been illustrated in many
graceful and noble poems by many loved
and honored poets : by Lowell also ; but in
the ordinary acceptation of the meaning and
use of poetry he is but one of several eminent masters, each having his own great
merits ; while in this new field he is wholly
without a rival, — the sole laureate of the

native, unlettered speech, and the exemplar of the mother-wit of New England. The few characters in his dramas are complementary, or perhaps, as he himself suggests, "humorously identical under a seeming incongruity." The Rev. Mr. Wilbur expresses "the more cautious element of the New England character and its pedantry," as Hosea Biglow does "its homely commonsense vivified and heated by conscience.... Finding that I needed some one as a mouthpiece of the mere drollery, . . . I invented Mr. Sawin for the clown of my little puppet show."

The introduction to the series is a learned and masterly account of the dialect, — as a legitimate derivative of the spoken English of the Elizabethan age, — and a protest against the prevalent "fine writing," as tending to weaken prose and stifle poetry. He defends certain extravagances in speech (lamented by purists) as being evidences of "intensity and picturesqueness, symptoms of the imaginative faculty in full health and strength." He says, "The first postulate of an original literature is that a people should use their language instinctively and unconsciously. . . . Even Burns contrived to write very poor verse and prose in English. Vulgarisms are often only poetry in the egg."

The whole essay is pervaded by the intense individuality of genius. After enduring the petulance and assumption of philologists, and the canal-water flow of conservators of the purity of English, this fresh and original discussion is as charming and exhilarating as a day in the woods in spring.

CHAUCER-BOCCACCIO.

"Fitz Adam's Story" was printed in the "Atlantic" for January, 1867, but has not yet been included in any "complete" edition. A note informs us that it was intended as a part of a longer poem to be called "The Nooning." It stands like the wing of a projected edifice, waiting for the main structure to give it countenance.

This poem has many traits in common with the best of the "Biglow Papers." Like them, it is exuberant in feeling and secular in tone; and its movement is breezy, out-of-doors, and natural, — as different from the precise, conscious, and scholastic manner as the glowing energy of a sermon by Beecher is from the marmorean elegance of Everett. The poem is not wholly in a comic vein. The portrait of Fitz Adam himself is a masterpiece, an instantaneous view of a complexity of character and motive, —genius and whim kneaded together and made real flesh and blood. In fact, the author uses the whole gamut, and has the ready chords for sentiment and poetical description as well as for the swift *parlando* of wit and the unrestrained chorus of fun.

Fitz Adam tells us, —

> " Without a Past you lack that southern wall
> O'er which the vines of Poesy should crawl."

He pays his homage to our great romancer : —

> " You have one story-teller worth a score
> Of dead Boccaccios, — nay, add twenty more,
> A hawthorn asking spring's most southern breath,
> And him you 're freezing pretty well to death."

He takes us to Shebagog County, where the summer idlers

> " Dress to see Nature in a well-bred way,
> As 't were Italian opera, or play,
> Encore the sunrise, (if they 're out of bed,)
> And pat the Mighty Mother on the head."

Fond of the frontiers-men and their natural ways, he puts them in a line : —

> " The shy, wood-wandering brood of character."

He paints the landlord of the rustic inn. The picture seems as deep-lined and lasting as one of Chaucer's. We see the tanned cheeks and the " brambly breast," and how

> " a hedge of gray
> Upon his brawny throat leaned every way
> About an Adam's apple that beneath
> Bulged like a bowlder from a furzy heath."

The landlord gives an axiom for the kitchen, for which the epicure will hold him in affectionate remembrance : —

> " Nothin' riles me (I pledge my fastin' word),
> Like cookin' out the natur' of a bird."

Fitz Adam describes the solemn parlor in a way to raise a sympathetic chill in the reader : —

> " Where the black sofa with its horse-hair pall
> Gloomed like the bier for Comfort's funeral."

The bar is painted as if by Teniers, with its great wood-fire, and the coals in which was heating

> " the loggerhead whose hissing dip,
> Timed by nice instinct, creamed the mug of flip."

Then follows the encounter of teamsters' wits, and the sketch of Deacon Bitters, a mean and avaricious wretch whose tricks brought him to a sulphureous end. The audacity of the story is forgotten in its absurdly comic keeping. It is a modern Canterbury Tale.

THE PROFESSOR SUPPLANTS THE POET.

Though Harvard College and its successive classes of students and the learned world have been indebted to the critical

labors of Lowell, yet mankind at large have
been more interested in the original creations
of his genius. The effect of his engrossing
and protracted studies has been to make
more prominent the philosophic tone in his
verse. To him who is day by day wrestling
with the stern problems of Dante, or con-
templating the creations of Shakespeare,
there may come a high and noble mastery
of philosophy and art. But the period in
which the poet delights in outdoor life —
when his soul feels God in nature, and floats
in the ocean of analogies between the real
and the ideal world — is the period in which
his best poems are born. The work of the
great critic may imply the rarer power;
but mankind cherishes more the pictures
of Beaver Brook and Appledore, the song of
bobolinks, the joy of spring, and the loves
of Huldys and Zekles. Lowell's mind underwent a change also in the loss of his
heroic nephews and other near relatives in
the war. This is painfully evident in the

poem before quoted. There were to be
fewer birds and blossoms thenceforth. The
awful lessons of Divine Providence were
such as to sadden the most joyous or the
most religious of men. Under such afflic-
tions, particularly after life has passed its
meridian, it is impossible to feel anew the
ecstatic thrills in the presence of nature;
the mind grows introspective, ponders the
deep questions of Job and his friends, and
forgets the external world.

UNDER THE WILLOWS.

It will be seen that the period in which
Lowell's most popular works appeared ended
with the late war. They cannot be classified,
however, in a chronological order, because
he sometimes allowed a considerable period
to pass before giving a poem to the public.
The collection entitled "Under the Willows,"
published in 1869, contains "A Winter-Even-
ing Hymn to my Fire," printed originally
in "Putnam's Monthly" fifteen years before.

"Fitz Adam's Story," which has just been considered, belongs to a similar period, as do the gay and characteristic acknowledgment of Mr. John Bartlett's trout, and the well-known pathetic ballad, "The First Snow-Fall." In the variety of subjects, the perfect keeping of the style of each, the power of suggesting a landscape or an image by a single phrase, and in the mature and perfect art, this volume has a rightful place among the chief intellectual works of the century.

It is difficult to convey an adequate impression of these poems, because it is seldom that the striking paragraphs are separable. The address "To the Muse" is the most subtile and delicate in treatment; and "Villa Franca" and "The Washers of the Shroud" are the strongest in thought. Two stanzas are quoted from "Villa Franca" which show a singular prophetic power. The poem was written in 1859, at the time of the meeting of the three emperors, when Napoleon III. appeared to be as firmly established as his great and long-descended compeers.

VILLA FRANCA.

"We shall see him come and gone,
  This second-hand Napoleon.
   .   .   .   .

" We saw the elder Corsican,
  And Clotho muttered as she span,
  While crowned lackeys bore the train,
  Of the pinchbeck Charlemagne :
  ' Sister, stint not length of thread !
  Sister, stay the scissors dread !
  On Saint Helen's granite bleak,
  Hark, the vulture whets his beak !'
    Spin, spin, Clotho, spin !
    Lachesis, twist ! and, Atropos, sever !
    In the shadow, year out, year in,
    The silent headsman waits forever.

   .   .   .   .   .   .

" The Bonapartes, we know their bees
  That wade in honey red to the knees ;
  Their patent reaper, its sheaves sleep sound
  In dreamless garners underground :
  We know false glory's spendthrift race
  Pawning nations for feathers and lace ;
  It may be short, it may be long,
  ' 'T is reckoning-day !' sneers unpaid Wrong.
    Spin, spin, Clotho, spin !
    Lachesis, twist ! and, Atropos, sever !
    In the shadow, year out, year in,
    The silent headsman waits forever."

One small poem is printed entire, as a rare specimen of aphoristic art.

FOR AN AUTOGRAPH.

Though old the thought and oft exprest,
'T is his at last who says it best, —
I 'll try my fortune with the rest.

Life is a leaf of paper white
Whereon each one of us may write
His word or two, and then comes night.

"Lo, time and space enough," we cry,
"To write an epic ! " so we try
Our nibs upon the edge, and die.

Muse not which way the pen to hold,
Luck hates the slow and loves the bold,
Soon come the darkness and the cold.

Greatly begin ! though thou have time
But for a line, be that sublime, —
Not failure, but low aim, is crime.

Ah, with what lofty hope we came !
But we forget it, dream of fame,
And scrawl, as I do here, a name.

As a critic, Lowell has been more unsparing upon his own productions than upon the works of others. Genius and Taste are twinborn; the one creates, the other tests. Many a day Genius produces nothing that Taste will allow. Taste corrects or blots out, so as to leave nothing that Time will destroy. Happy is the Genius with whom Taste continues to dwell as a friend and helper. Too often he goes over to the enemy, and sits in judgment with the reviewers.

Some of his later poems have, as in Emerson's "Test," been hung in the wind and smelted in a pot,

> "Till the meaning was more white
> Than July's meridian light.
> Sunshine cannot bleach the snow,
> Nor Time unmake what poets know."

METAPHYSICAL SUBTILTY IN POETRY.

The original traits of Lowell's genius are unmistakable; and, in spite of the gravity of his later poems, the reader often comes upon the turns of thought which marked his verse twenty years before. But along with the continued likeness there has been a slowly growing divergence. In the development of a scholar and poet we expect to see the evidences of maturing powers, varied experience, and mastery of expression; that is to say, force, wisdom, and skill are the natural gains of twenty years. This is true in the case of Lowell; but what is more remarkable is the steady lifting of his intellectual horizon, and the spiritualizing of thought, so that, as in the celestial mechanics, words become the symbols of ideas that reach towards the infinite. This is considered to be in the domain of Emerson, but Lowell is sometimes more transcendental even than the great poet-philosopher himself.

In "The Foot-Path" the reader begins with a view that is within his not infrequent experience : —

> "It mounts athwart the windy hill
>   Through sallow slopes of upland bare,
> And Fancy climbs with foot-fall still
>   Its narrowing curves that end in air."

But the poet's aerial way only begins where mortal vision ends. As stanza succeeds musical stanza, the mind follows clews and glimpses, conscious of sensations for which there are no words, and of an upward motion into a realm where ideas are as fluent as air, and as impalpable. Read this exquisite but tantalizing poem to any chance-gathering of well-bred people, and observe their puzzled expression! To some it will appear a musical stream, without ripple and without meaning. Few will climb the poet's stairway to the heaven of thought!

Humboldt said that the vegetation upon the sides of Chimborazo exhibits at successive elevations all the characteristic flora from the equator to the arctic circle: the boundless luxuriance of the tropics at the base, and the eternal ice of the pole at the summit. Poetry likewise comprehends many zones. Its lower level is in scenes of lavish beauty, and it concerns itself in the joy of the senses in external nature. Higher up there are fewer flowers and hardier growths, but "purer air and broader view." Still higher are the brown and lichened steeps that tax strength and demand self-denial. Above, and reaching into the infinite sky, is the silent peak, inaccessible, eternal.

COMMEMORATION ODE.

The Commemoration Ode (July 21, 1865) naturally succeeds the poignant grief of the later "Biglow Papers." The dedication is one that only a poet could have written: "To the ever sweet and shining memory of the ninety-three sons of Harvard College who have died for their country in the war of nationality." In the privately printed edition of the poem the names of eight of the poet's kindred are given. The nearest in blood are his nephews, General Charles Russell Lowell, killed at Winchester, Lieutenant James Jackson Lowell, at Seven Pines, and Captain William Lowell Putnam,

at Ball's Bluff. Another relative was the heroic Colonel Robert G. Shaw, who fell in the
assault upon Fort Wagner. The Commemoration services took place in the open air, in
the presence of a great assembly. Prominent among the speakers were Major-General
Meade, the hero of Gettysburg, and Major-
General Devens. The wounds of the war
were still fresh and bleeding, and the interest
of the occasion was deep and thrilling. The
summer afternoon was drawing to its close
when the poet began the recital of the ode.
No living audience could for the first time
follow with intelligent appreciation the de-
livery of such a poem. To be sure, it had
its obvious strong points and its sonorous
charms; but, like all the later poems of the
author, it is full of condensed thought and
requires study. The reader to-day finds
many passages whose force and beauty es-
caped him during the recital, yet the effect
of the poem at the time was overpowering.
The face of the poet, always singularly ex-

pressive, was on this occasion almost trans-
figured, — glowing, as if with an inward
light. It was impossible to look away from
it. Our age has furnished many great historic scenes, but this Commemoration com-
bined the elements of grandeur and pathos,
and produced an impression as lasting as life.
Of the merits of the ode it is perhaps too
soon to speak. In nobility of sentiment and
sustained power it appears to take rank
among the first in the language. To us,
with the memories of the war in mind, it
seems more beautiful and of a finer quality
than the best of Dryden's. What the people
of the coming centuries will say, who knows?
We only know that the auditors, scholars and
soldiers alike, were dissolved in admiration
and tears.

TWO FRIENDS.

As the people were dispersing, a fresh-
looking, active, and graceful man of middle
age, in faultless attire, met the poet with an

outstretched hand. There was a hearty greeting on both sides, — so hearty, that one wonders how it could have happened between two Bostonians, whose marble manners the public knows so well from our recent fashionable novels. It was not the formal touch of gloved hands, but an old-fashioned energetic "shake;" and it was accompanied by spontaneous, half-articulated words (such as the heart translates without a lexicon), while eager and misty eyes met each other. The new-comer was William W. Story, the sculptor and poet. — "When did you come over?" — "I landed at Boston this morning. I had heard you were to read a poem; there was just time to make the trip, and here I am." — "And so you have come from Rome merely to hear me recite an ode? Well, it is just like you."

THE CATHEDRAL. — CONSERVATISM.

"The Cathedral" is a profound meditation upon a great theme. A poet is not held to the literal meaning of the motto he selects, but the lines prefixed to this poem [1] are strongly significant of a growing conservatism in thought. "Not at all do we set our wits against the gods. The traditions of the fathers, and those of equal date which we possess, no reasoning shall overthrow; not even if through lofty minds it discovers wisdom." This is perhaps a fair indication of the feeling of the poem. The incidents of the day at Chartres are unimportant, except in connection with the poet's admiration for Gothic architecture, and his musings upon the associations of the cathedral, the old worship, the old reverence, and the old ways.

It would seem that the intellectual movement in which the poet had been borne on for so many years was latterly becoming too rapid and tumultuous, according to his thinking, — ready to plunge into an abyss, in fact. In particular, it may be observed that, though

[1] Euripides, Bacchæ, 196–199.

the physical aspect of evolution had engaged his attention, as it has that of all intellectual men, and had commanded, perhaps, a startled and dubious assent, yet his strong spiritual nature recoiled in horror from the material-istic application of the doctrine to the origin of things. Force could never be to him the equivalent of spirit, nor law the substitute for God. In conversation once upon the " prom-ise-and-potency " phrases of Tyndall, he ex-claimed with energy, " Let whoever wishes to, believe that the idea of Hamlet or Lear was developed from a clod ; I will not."

A couplet from " The Foot-Path " makes a similar protest against the theory of the uni-verse which leaves out a Creator : —

> " And envy Science not her feat
> To make a twice-told tale of God."

Intimations of the Berkeleyan theory ap-pear in " The Cathedral," not as matters of belief, but of speculation. But the granitic basis of the poem is the generally received doctrine of the being of God, — of His works

THE WAVERLEY OAKS.

and His dealings with men. The clear purpose is seen by the attentive reader, although at times through a haze of poetic diction. Its strong points are in the simplicity and suggestiveness of its illustrations, its firm hold upon the past, and its tranquil repose in the care of Divine Providence. The style is for the most part scholastic, nervous, and keen-edged. There are some lovely rural pictures near the beginning, so characteristic that if they were done in color we should not need to look at the corner for the " J. R. L. pinx^t."

The episode of the two Englishmen at Chartres, who, on account of the poet's full and ruddy beard, mistook him for a Frenchman, and endeavored to engage him as a guide, is a piece of drollery that one would prefer to see in a sketch by Artemus Ward or Mark Twain.

"My beard translated me to hostile French;
So they, desiring guidance in the town,
Half condescended to my baser sphere,
And, clubbing in one mess their lack of phrase,
Set their best man to grapple with the Gaul.

9

> ' Esker vous ate a nabitang?' he asked ;
> ' I never ate one ; are they good ?' asked I ;
> Whereat they stared, then laughed, and we were friends."

The wit is perhaps bright, but the passage is painfully incongruous. It is true the old cathedrals have carvings of grotesque comedy, but they are in stone, and are not obtrusive. This appears to be the single thought out of place in the high serenity of a philosophic poem.

Two instances of the harmony of sound and sense are quite remarkable. One is the description of the falling of an ash-leaf, —

> " Balancing softly earthward without wind," —

an inimitably perfect line. The other suggests the swinging of a bell-blossom : —   .

> " As to a bee the new campanula's
> Illuminate seclusion swung in air."

A few lines and passages may be quoted with advantage : —

> " I found mine eyes
> Confronted with the minster's vast repose.
> Silent and gray as forest-leaguered cliff
> Left inland by the ocean's slow retreat.
> .   .   .   .

(*Of Gothic Architecture.*)

But ah ! this other, this that never ends,
Still climbing, luring fancy still to climb,
As full of morals half-divined as life,
Graceful, grotesque, with ever new surprise
Of hazardous caprices sure to please,
Heavy as nightmare, airy-light as fern,
Imagination's very self in stone !

. . . .

Far up the great bells wallowed in delight,
Tossing their clangors o'er the heedless town.

. . . .

Use can make sweet the peach's shady side,
That only by reflection tastes of sun.

. . . .

. . . on the sliding Eure,
Whose listless leisure suits the quiet place,
Lisping among his shallows homelike sounds
At Concord and by Bankside heard before.

. . . .

Blessèd the natures shored on every side
With landmarks of hereditary thought !

. . . .

Now Calvin and Servetus at one board
Snuff in grave sympathy a milder roast,
And o'er their claret settle Comte unread.
Fagot and stake were desperately sincere :
Our cooler martyrdoms are done in types.

. . . .

Thou beautiful Old Time, now hid away
In the Past's valley of Avilion,
Haply, like Arthur, till thy wound be healed,
Then to reclaim the sword and crown again !
Thrice beautiful to us ; perchance less fair
To who possessed thee, as a mountain seems
To dwellers round its bases but a heap
Of barren obstacle that lairs the storm
And the avalanche's silent bolt holds back
Leashed with a hair, — meanwhile some far-off clown,
Hereditary delver of the plain,
Sees it an unmoved vision of repose,
Nest of the morning, and conjectures there
The dance of streams to idle shepherds' pipes,
And fairer habitations softly hung
On breezy slopes, or hid in valleys cool,
For happier men."

True to its name, " The Cathedral " is a grand poem, at once solid and imaginative, nobly ornate, but with a certain austerity of design, uplifting and impressive. These edifices are perhaps the most wonderful productions of mind ; but they are gloomy also, and in some moods strike a chill to the very marrow.

CONCORD, CAMBRIDGE, VIRGINIA.

Three odes have since appeared, written for important occasions, all characterized by a lofty tone of sentiment and stately poetic diction. The first is one read at Concord, April 19, 1875; the next is that read at Cambridge, under the Washington Elm, July 3d in the same year; the third, an ode for the Fourth of July, 1876. The Concord ode contains the most exquisite music, and shows the most evident inspiration. The Cambridge ode is remarkable for its noble tribute to Washington and to the historic Commonwealth of Virginia. The last is beautiful also, and strong, but scarcely so clear and fortunate as the others. But these, with the Commemoration Ode, are an Alpine group, an undying part of our national literature.

CLASSICISM.

The poetry called classic in our time has little vitality. The poems of Matthew Arnold, for instance, cold and correct as mort-

uary tributes, differ from pensive prose only
in respect to metrical form.   In this sense
Lowell's poems are not classic : they are in-
stinct with life.   They show marks of care ;
but the care has been bestowed less upon
melody than upon condensation and energy.
The earlier poems were more melodious.   Instances enough could be given, but two stanzas from "The Dandelion" must serve : —

> " Then think I of deep shadows on the grass, —
> Of meadows where in sun the cattle graze,
>   Where, as the breezes pass,
> The gleaming rushes lean a thousand ways, —
>   Of leaves that slumber in a cloudy mass,
> Or whiten in the wind, — of waters blue
>   That from the distance sparkle through
>   Some woodland gap, — and of a sky above,
>   Where one white cloud like a stray lamb doth move.
>
> " My childhood's earliest thoughts are linked with thee ;
> The sight of thee calls back the robin's song,
>   Who, from the dark old tree
> Beside the door, sang clearly all day long,
>   And I, secure in childish piety,
> Listened as if I heard an angel sing
>   With news from heaven, which he could bring
>   Fresh every day to my untainted ears
>   When birds and flowers and I were happy peers."

This devotion to the force and beauty of ideas is everywhere to be seen. The poet will not give up a harsh word, nor elide an unmusical huddle of consonants, if any strength would be lost thereby. A stanza from "Beaver Brook" will illustrate this : —

> "Swift slips Undine along the race
> Unheard, and then, with flashing bound,
> Floods the dull wheel with light and grace,
> And, laughing, hunts the loath drudge round."

Sibilants and gutturals may delay the fastidious reader, but when the lines are finished he will think only of the immortal beauty of the image.

Pure poetry, like the subtile essences of the chemist, is rarely seen but in combination. In itself it is thought sublimed, remote from demonstration, persuasion, or narration. The influences of the strong and serviceable qualities of mind are apt to be felt at times in the verse even of great poets, — like stains of iron in marble; so that the wholly fortunate or perfect specimens are

few. The common error is in lapsing into
philosophic discourse, or indulging in reflec-
tive or hortatory asides. Something of this
tendency appears in parts of Lowell's odes,
dimming their lustre, and even tending to
obscurity. There is nothing in them obscure
to a well-trained mind; but unfortunately
not all minds are so trained as to dissolve
his thought from out the richly incrusted
diction. So it remains that the stronger
poems of Lowell are beyond the comprehension of all but cultivated readers.

A wonderful sifter is Time. "Complete"
works will shrink. Stanzas or even whole
poems may drop out, but the best will be
preserved. And it is difficult to believe that
an intelligent reader, whether in the year
2000 or 3000, will come upon certain poems
of Lowell without a thrill of sympathy and
delight.

THE PROSE OF POETS.

The prose writings of poets are rarely conspicuous for masculine qualities. The Laureate has been heard only in numbers, as if, like an operatic performer, he were theoretically incapable of any but musical speech. If his predecessor had similarly refrained from prosaic utterances, he would have been the gainer, — and the world too. Byron wrote natural and effective prose, but without either trained ratiocination, scholarly allusion, or finish. Cowper's letters are models of ease and grace. Southey's prose is magnificent; his poetry? — Really one questions whether he was a poet at all. "Thalaba" seems as unreal as a Wagnerian legend or an Ossianic wraith. Milton alone holds a fixed place among the greatest of poets and the ablest of prose writers.

The prose works of Lowell consist of the "Fireside Travels," already referred to, and three volumes of essays, published in 1870,

1871, and 1876. Of these, the one entitled
" My Study Windows" will be found most
interesting to general readers. The other
two are entitled " Among My Books," and
are of a purely literary character. A large
number of his essays have appeared in magazines and reviews, and have not been as yet
reprinted.

It is a common but baseless supposition
that the poetic faculty must exist singly ; as
if the cranium, like a flower-pot, could hold
but one plant. It is true that great poets are
rarely men of affairs ; but every genius is an
absolutely new combination of traits and
powers, and no one knows the possibilities.
Four arts owned Michelangelo master, and
he was almost equally great in all. We have
seen that in the mind of Lowell there is an
unfailing spring of analogy and suggestion,
and a power of illustrating subtile and profound thoughts. And side by side with this
undeniable poetic power is to be seen the
solid understanding, the ready wit, and the

practical sagacity that are more commonly the birthright of unpoetic men. It is as if the souls of Shelley and Ben Franklin had blended. The poet leads, but the man of ethereal imagination and the man of sturdy force are one.

The prose of a true poet, if one reflects upon it, must have some marked peculiarities. That which is of the essence of poetry is not in its musical cadence, not in its shining adjectives and epithets: it is in substance as well as in form different from the ordinary productions of mind. And as the power of appreciation is really rare, though often assumed, the distinctive prose of a poet is necessarily quite removed from general apprehension. The difficulty lies in following the movement of the poetic mind, which is by nature erratic, if measured by prose standards, — taking many things for granted which the slower-footed expect to see put down in order, — and often supplying the omission of a premiss in a logical statement, or the want of a formal description, by a single flashing word. Those people who need to have poetry expounded to them, will require similar help to understand the prose of poets. "Villa Franca," "The Foot-Path," "The Washers of the Shroud," and "The Cathedral" will never be easy of comprehension; such poems make drafts upon the knowledge and the insight of even superior minds. Certain of Lowell's essays — especially those upon Shakespeare, Dante, and Milton — will be fully appreciated by only a limited number of readers in any generation.

LOWELL'S PROSE.

It is not wonderful that this rich and imaginative prose, permeated as it is with the essence of poetry, should have called forth unfavorable comment and objurgation. Professor Wilkinson, some years ago, wrote a series of labored articles in a popular magazine, which it was expected were to demolish our poet's reputation as an essayist.

Perhaps some characteristic sentences will better illustrate our meaning as to the divergence between the poetic and the prosaic mind.

Of Wordsworth, Lowell says: —

" His longer poems are Egytian sand wastes, with here and there an oasis of exquisite greenery, a grand image, Sphynx-like, half buried in drifting commonplaces, or the Pompey's Pillar of some towering thought."

How absurd this is! What has Wordsworth to do with Egypt and the Sphynx and Pompey's Pillar? — though, to be sure, one sees what he *would* say. If it had been the critical professor who had to give the opinion, it might have been phrased like this: " His longer poems are flat and dreary, with here and there a spot of human interest, — some originally fine image, half covered with meaningless words, or some striking thought that holds the attention."

This is plain sailing: no nonsense about it. The idea is the same, and everybody can

understand it.   In a similar perspicuous manner the "practical" critic might tell us of
Milton's style: "Milton has a grand manner.
The sentences move slowly and with stateli-
ness.   He borrowed phrases from poets and
writers of all times; and these epithets are
continually coming in the way, obscuring
the clear thought."

This is the way Lowell has it : —

> "Milton's manner is very grand.   It is slow, it
> is stately, moving as in triumphal procession, with
> music, with historic banners, with spoils from every
> time and every region ; — and captive epithets like
> huge Sicambrians,[1] thrust their broad shoulders
> between us and the pomp they decorate."

Of course this is all wrong.   Burke, also,
ought to undergo revision.   If a practical
person were to undertake it, it is probable
that the twelve volumes of Burke could be
compressed into three or four, simply leaving

---

[1] "Te cæde gaudentis Sicambri
Compositis venerantur armis."
                    Hor. Lib. IV. Carm. XIV.

out useless images, and the like. The staple of "Modern Painters" could be printed in one duodecimo. Following the same plan, each of Hawthorne's romances could be got into the limits of a magazine story; and, by eliminating the fine writing and metaphysics, they would be as easily understood as Peter Parley or the Rollo Books.

The prose essays of Lowell [1] cover a wide range of thought and observation, but all have the inevitable family likeness. Mention has been made of the delightful "Fireside Travels." Of a similar tone are "My Garden Acquaintance," "A Good Word for Winter," and "On a Certain Condescension in Foreigners." The last is a specimen of pure irony, keen as a Damascus blade, and finished to the utmost. It is doubtful if there is another essay in modern English superior in power, wit, and adroitness. The essay upon Lessing is a charming

---

[1] "Among My Books," 2 vols.; "My Study Windows," 1 vol.

piece of writing, full of bright passages, but interesting mainly to scholars. "New England Two Centuries Ago" is an historical article, in which the Puritans and Pilgrims are boldly sketched, — neither unduly flattered nor summarily condemned.

GOLD IN QUARTZ.

A few additional specimens of poetical imagery are quoted : —

"The commentary on Shakespeare by Gervinus reminds one of the Roman Campagna, penetrated underground in all directions by strange winding caverns, the work of human borers in search of we know not what. Above are the divine poet's larks and daisies, his incommunicable skies, his broad prospects of life and nature ; and meanwhile our Teutonic *teredo* worms his way below, and offers to be our guide into an obscurity of his own creating."

"The German Language has such a fatal genius for going stern-foremost, for yawing, and for not minding the helm without some ten minutes' notice in advance, that he must be a great sailor indeed who can safely make it the vehicle for anything but imperishable commodities."

" Wordsworth wrote too much to write always well; for it is not a great Xerxes-army of words, but a compact Greek ten thousand that march safely down to posterity."

" The best of Schiller's lyrical poems find no match in modern verse for rapid energy, — the very axles of language kindling with swiftness."

" Chaucer's best tales run on like one of our inland rivers, sometimes hastening a little and turning upon themselves in eddies that dimple without retarding the current; sometimes loitering smoothly, while here and there a quiet thought, a tender feeling, a pleasant image, a golden-hearted verse, opens quietly as a water-lily, to float on the surface without breaking it into ripple."

As some stress has been laid upon the poetical ornaments of the style, or rather, it might be said, upon the diffusion of golden grains of poetry through the quartz of prose, it should be again stated more emphatically that the literary essays are chiefly valuable

10

for their clear thought and their varied and splendid learning. Let any student read the essay on Chaucer, and then consider where he can find its parallel! It is not merely a specimen of magnificent writing: it is a compact and lucid account of the origin and growth of English poetry, with a series of brilliant characterizations; and it is such an account as no historian or critic has made. The antiquarian scholars have the literal facts at command; but no one possessed of the necessary erudition has had at the same time the power of raising literary annals into æsthetic history. Taine's treatment of the same period is characteristically pretentious, sentimental, and shallow.

We can see evidences of the same thorough preparation in the other essays. Lowell has never trusted to "style" to carry him through: not Dryasdust himself could have had the details of the subject more at command. So it may be asserted, in general, that each essay contains the latest thought as

well as the most complete information. All
of them are redolent of learning, and all have
an incommunicable flavor. The treatment
of Dryden is able and masterly; albeit his
numerous apostasies are too leniently dealt
with. Spenser is the subject of an essay
scarcely inferior to that upon Chaucer, and
equally indispensable to students of English
literature.

Dante seems to be a literature in himself,
and none but devoted students have the right
to judge him, or the essays upon him. It
may be observed that most who have
studied Dante profoundly have become in
the end conservatives in religion, if not Cath-
olics. The circle of his admirers is necessarily small. Lowell's essay is evidently
a tribute of affection ; and as the estimate of a poet, it is worthy of respectful
study. It exhibits the results of protracted
thought upon the highest themes which have
occupied the mind of man.

But of all the series, the one entitled

" Shakespeare Once More " is doubtless the best. There will always be some new light radiating from the works of the greatest of poets, and each succeeding generation will be satisfied only with its own estimate ; but the most comprehensive estimate of Shakespeare to-day is Lowell's.

The essays of Lowell, it must be admitted, have not the elements of general popularity. Criticism in its highest form is not attractive except to thinkers. The few essays that are widely read — like Macaulay's and Carlyle's — are studies of historical characters, or of great epochs, with graphic personal descriptions and parallels, treated in a highly-wrought style of rhetoric. In fact, the ordinary critical essays, unless there is a personal flavor in them, such as we perceive in Montaigne and in the " Autocrat of the Breakfast Table," are as short-lived as the reign of a London beauty. The changes in literary fashion soon make the critic obsolete. Except as curiosities, who cares now for the opinions of Lockhart, Jeffrey, Mackintosh, Gifford, and the rest? The tables are turned. Byron, Keats, Shelley, Coleridge, and Wordsworth now "compute" their reviewers. In general, it may be said that the quality which prevents the general appreciation of Lowell's prose is its exceeding richness. It is like cloth of gold, — too splendid and too cumbrous for every-day wear.

It is upon his poems that the sure foundation of Lowell's fame will rest. Some of them are the clear and fortunate expression of the noblest modern thought, and others are imbedded in the history of an eventful time. When the relative perspective of history is adjusted, Lincoln's proclamation of freedom to the slave will tower in importance. The elders are perhaps weary of the topic, but the vindication of the anti-slavery agitators and poets may be safely left to Time.

PERSONAL TRAITS AND ANECDOTES.

In person Lowell is of medium height, rather slender, but sinewy and active. His movements are deliberate rather than impulsive, indicating what athletes call staying qualities. His hair at maturity was dark auburn or ruddy chestnut in color, and his full beard rather lighter and more glowing in tint. The eyes of men of genius are seldom to be classified in ordinary terms, though it is said their prevailing color is gray. Colonel Higginson mentions Hawthorne's gray eyes; while the present writer, who once studied them attentively, found them mottled gray and brown, and at that time indescribably soft and winning. That they were sometimes *accipitral* we can readily believe. Lowell's eyes in repose have clear blue and gray tones, with minute dark mottlings. In expression they are strongly indicative of his moods. When fixed upon study, or while listening to serious discourse, they are grave

and penetrating; in ordinary conversation
they are bright and cheery; in moments of
excitement they have a wonderful lustre.
Nothing could be finer than his facial expression while telling a story or tossing a repartee.
The features are alive with intelligence; and
eyes, looks, and voice appear to be working
up dazzling effects in concert, like the finished
artists of the Comédie Française.

The wit of Hosea Biglow is the native wit
of Lowell, — instantaneous as lightning; and
Hosea's common sense is Lowell's birthright,
too. When the same man, moreover, can
extemporize chuckling puns, or blow out a
breath of poetical reverie as naturally as the
smoke from his pipe, the combination becomes almost marvellous. Other men may
have been as witty, though we recall but
three or four in our day; some may have
had a similar fund of wisdom mellowed with
humor; others have talked the staple of idyls,
and let off metaphors like soap-bubbles; but
Lowell combines in conversation the varied

powers of all. His resources are inexhausti-
ble. It is no wonder that he has been admired; for at his best he is one of the most
fascinating of men. There is but one com-
peer, — the immortal Autocrat, — and it
would be difficult and perhaps impossible to
draw a parallel between them.

Steele said of a lady, that to have known
and loved her was a liberal education. More
than one man who enjoyed Lowell's society
found that the wise and witty converse of
years did much to supply lamented defects
in his own study and training, and perhaps
warmed even late-flowering plants into blos-
som and fruitage. This also should be said,
that every man who has known Lowell well
considers him much greater than the aggre-
gate of his works. He always gives the impression of power in reserve, and of the
probability of still higher achievement.

He used to enter upon the long walks
which have aided in making him one of the
poets of nature with the keenest zest. There

was no quicker eye for a bird or squirrel, a rare flower or bush, and no more accurate ear for the songs or the commoner sounds of the forest. Evidences of this the reader will find in the "Study Windows." But those who have visited Fresh Pond, Clematis Brook, Love Lane, or the Waverley Oaks in his company remember an acuteness of vision and a delight in every form of beauty of which the essay gives no conception.

His habits have been scarcely methodical, — reading, correspondence, composition, exercise, and social converse coming often haphazard, — yet, being incapable of idleness, he has accomplished much. His reading has been enormous, covering the literature of many countries and times: from Marco Polo to Doctor Kane; from Piers Plowman to Swinburne; from the Christian Fathers to Channing; from Boccaccio and Cervantes to Thackeray; from Froissart to Motley; — and this has given him the materials indispensable to a great writer. His works show the effective use he has made of the intellectual treasures of the world.

Mrs. Hawthorne relates that before her husband completed "The Scarlet Letter" there was a visible *knot* in the muscles of his forehead, caused by the intensity of thought. When a great theme was in mind, Lowell used always to go to his desk with all his might. Like Sir Walter Raleigh, he could "toil terribly." It has been already mentioned that "Sir Launfal" was written in about two days. The production of a poem like "The Cathedral" or the Commemoration Ode taxed his faculties to the utmost, and always left him exhausted in body and mind. At such periods his wife and daughter, knowing his nature and needs, used various artifices to divert him, and prevent the strain becoming too tense.

THE WHIST CLUB.

Between 1850 and 1860, Lowell was not much in society, in the present restricted

sense of the word. Dinner parties and recep-
tions of the fashionable world appeared to
have little attraction for him. He never
enjoyed being lionized. In Cambridge there
were several men with whom he was on intimate terms, and to them he gave his society
ungrudgingly. Chief among these was his
brother-in-law, Dr. Estes Howe, a man of
liberal education and delightful social qualities. He is "The Doctor" referred to in the
preface to the "Fable for Critics." "The
Don" was a pleasant nickname for Mr. Robert
Carter, formerly Lowell's coadjutor in the
short-lived "Pioneer," and employed at that
time as secretary by Mr. Prescott, the historian. Carter was a remarkable man, prin-
cipally on account of his great reading and
retentive memory. He was an able writer
also, but he had read more out-of-the-way
things than any man living. Lowell used to
say that he would back Carter on a wager
to write off-hand an account of a journey
in the fifth century B. C. from Rome to

Babylon or Pekin, with descriptions of all
the peoples on the way. Carter lived at first
in a modest house near the Willows (celebrated in Lowell's verse), and afterwards in
Sparks Street, not far from the Riedesel
House. The Sparks Street house has associations such as belong to the tavern of
Kit North's friend Ambrose, — lacking, however, the overplus of toddy and the coarse-
ness which smirched the discourse of the
Blackwood coterie. Carter's house was often
a rendezvous for whist parties. But whist
was the least of the business or pleasure
of the evening. The new books, — or old
ones, — magazines, pictures, reminiscences,
and stories occupied the available intervals.
The silence and severity of Mrs. Battles was
unknown. Charles Lamb and his venerable
dame were often quoted by Lowell, but the
" rigor of the game " was a transparent joke.
When a story came to mind, or an epigram,
or double-shotted pun, the cards might wait;
when the story was told, or the puns had cor-

ruscated amid roars of laughter, the professor would blandly ask, " What are trumps ? "

Other players must rest in shadow. Two of them may be named in whom the reading world has an interest. One was John Bartlett, author of the book of " Familiar Quotations," a charming companion, and a man of refined taste. The other, who was the delight of all companies, was John Holmes, brother of the poet-professor. He was the songless poet, the silent Autocrat. It is difficult to say what he might have done if shut up with pen, ink, and paper; but he had the rarest humor and a genius for the unexpected. He always had the art of showing the *other side* of a statement, and of bringing a joke out of the impossible, like a conjurer.

Changes in the whist parties occurred, as was natural, owing to illness or absence ; but they continued for several years. The members are all living except Carter, who died in Cambridge about a year ago, universally regretted. May he rest in peace! The

recollections of that period form a bond not
to be sundered while life and thought continue.

Of the other friends of Lowell much might
be said if there were room. Some of them
are named in his books.

HINTS OF FRIENDSHIPS.

The edition of poems published in 1849
was affectionately dedicated to the eminent
painter, William Page. The second series
of the "Biglow Papers" was appropriately
inscribed to E. R. Hoar, who is

> "the Jedge, who covers with his hat
> More wit an' gumption an' shrewd Yankee sense
> Than there is mosses on an ole stone fence."

"Fireside Travels" is a series of letters ad-
dressed to Story, the sculptor. "Under the
Willows" bears the name of Charles Eliot
Norton, Professor of the History of Art at
Cambridge; "The Cathedral" is inscribed
to Mr. James T. Fields; "Three Memorial

Poems," to Mr. E. L. Godkin, editor of the
"Nation;" "My Study Windows," to Francis
J. Child, Professor of English Literature;
"Among My Books," to the present Mrs.
Lowell; the second volume of the same se-
ries to the illustrious Emerson. The chief
honor appears to have been paid to George
William Curtis, to whom the complete edi-
tion of poetical works is dedicated.

Arthur Hugh Clough, an English scholar
and poet, lived in Cambridge for about a
year (1855), and appears to have made a
deep impression upon Lowell. The un-
learned public knows little of Clough; but
all poets know the author of "The Bothie"
and "*Qua Cursum Ventus,*" and cultivated
people know the charming memoir of the
author by Professor Norton. He had a
beautiful, spiritual face and delicate, shy
manners; such a face and such manners as
are dimly seen in morning dreams. One
may be sure that such a rare being, if real
flesh and blood, would at some time be found

at Elmwood. Clough strongly advised Lowell to continue and develop the Yankee pastorals. In the introduction to the "Biglow Papers," Lowell says, *apropos* of the approval of friends: "With a feeling too tender and grateful to be mixed with any vanity, I mention as one of these the late A. II. Clough, who more than any one of those I have known (no longer living), except Hawthorne, impressed me with the constant presence of that indefinable thing we call genius."

The artists Stillman and Rowse were frequent visitors. Many of their pictures and sketches adorn Lowell's house.

` Cranch the poet and painter was a frequent and welcome visitor. President Felton was a stanch friend, and had great delight in Lowell's society. He and his brother-in-law, Agassiz, were alike hearty and natural men, fond of social pleasure, and manifesting the unaffected simplicity of children. Few men have won such deserved distinction in science and letters, and retained the freshness

of youthful feeling. At the club, Agassiz
was generally the centre of interest; for his
vast knowledge enabled him always to fur-
nish some ready and pertinent analogue.

Longfellow's house is but a short distance
from Elmwood, perhaps a quarter of a mile;
and the relations of the two poets have
always been intimate, as every observant
reader knows. Holmes lives in Boston; but
he was a frequent visitor in Cambridge at
the old house near the college, especially
while his mother lived. Lowell always paid
tribute to the consummate art and finish of
his friendly rival's verses, and to the vigor
and freshness of his style. The father of,
Dr. Holmes was a stout Orthodox clergyman;
Lowell's father was a mild and conservative
Unitarian. The Autocrat has developed into
a liberal, and our poet has been growing
more conservative, until now the relative
positions of the sons are nearly the reverse
of those of their fathers.

11

A CHARACTER.

Among the strange and remarkable people
that come to mind, Count Gurowski may
be mentioned. That brilliant and eccentric
man, in exile from his beloved Russia, was
engaged to deliver a course of lectures on
the civil law at the University. His habit
of unsparing censure soon got him into difficulty. The tongue which Russian nobles and
dames had dreaded *would* wag in Cambridge.
" Humbug" and " ass" were the mildest
terms he could find for some of the professors. His engagement was terminated, and
he shortly after disappeared. His singular
figure, his undaunted look, and his old-world
garments had made him a conspicuous object,
and he was missed. He was too proud to
ask for help, even for a sixpence. He pre-
ferred to starve. The generous Carter un-
dertook to look him up, and after a long
search found him digging in Hovey's nursery
grounds, at a dollar a day. He was wretched,

because old and unused to manual labor.
Carter took him to his house, and kept him
until some turn of fortune put the former
statesman and diplomatist on his feet again.
While he was at Carter's house a meeting of
the whist club occurred. Gurowski could
not say enough to Carter's friends of his
gratitude to the man who he declared had
saved his life. But in the course of the evening he said a great deal more. He attacked
everybody and everything. He combated
modern philosophy, scouted modern history,
and belittled modern poets. He was the
autocrat of all the Russias, and of mankind
in general. The lustre of his remaining eye.
(its fellow had been quenched in a duel) was
fascinating, and held his audience like Coleridge's Ancient Mariner. He bore down upon
the company like a full-rigged ship in a trade
wind, with all sails set. He would have no
contradiction. *Sic volo, sic jubeo.* Lowell
interposed now and then some bright and
apposite remarks, but Gurowski tolerated no

criticism or qualification. In the conflict of impetuous talk he was the Missouri bearing the current of the clearer and gentler Mississippi away to the opposite shore. His command of English, like Kossuth's, was miraculous, and the foreign accent was an attraction rather than impediment. But, of course, he was arbitrary and unjust to the last degree; and his triumph was not one of logic, for he talked for victory only. Such an exhibition was an experience of a lifetime. To be sure, it settled no facts nor principles, but it gave one an idea of the vast resources of a great mind under the guidance of a moody and wayward temper.

EDMUND QUINCY.

Edmund Quincy, son of the eminent president of Harvard, a man of education, taste, and wealth, was one of the foremost of the early abolitionists, and a ready and industrious writer upon the great question of his day. He was an early and intimate friend

of Lowell, and their visits were frequent.
Mr. Quincy had a large and comfortable
house, of the style of a century ago, at
Dedham, near the Charles. There was a
noble grove of pine-trees in the rear, ex-
tending to the river's edge. The estate was
called Bankside. Mr. Quincy is commemo-
rated in a fine poem under this title. There
is a reference to it, also, in "The Cathedral." Mr. Quincy took a warm interest
in the "Atlantic," having been one of the
original coterie of fourteen. He contributed no long articles; but several book
notices are still remembered for their pungent wit and epigrammatic force. He died
a few years ago, and it is permitted now
to say that few more elegant and accomplished men have ever been reared in Massachusetts. His manners were courtly and
refined, never cold or formal. His address
was graceful, and his courtesy unfailing.
Lowell used to say that, if we had an aris-
tocracy, Quincy would be a duke. A visit

to Bankside in the old days was something to be remembered.

BEGINS PUBLIC LIFE AT THE TOP.

In the course of this sketch there has been little attempt to follow order. The events of Lowell's life since 1860 have been few. The important dates are the dates of his books. One year has been like another, passed at the same residence, cheered by the same friends, engrossed in the same studies and pleasures. He visited Europe with Mrs. Lowell in 1873. He had never held office, not even that of justice of the peace; and though he has always had a warm interest in public affairs, he has not been a politician. It was therefore with some surprise as well as gratification that his friends heard of his appointment as Minister to Spain. He had been offered the Austrian mission, and had declined it; but some good spirit, perhaps Mr. Howells (a relative of President Hayes), suggested that Vienna was perhaps not the place to attract a scholar and poet, and that Madrid would be preferable, even with a smaller salary. After the retirement of Mr. Welsh, minister to England, Mr. Lowell was transferred to London. His reception in the metropolis of letters and of English-speaking people has been in the highest degree cordial and honorable.

He still holds his rank as professor at Cambridge, evidently expecting to resume his duties there. Perhaps in the Indian summer of his life he may put his heart into a poem that will be even more worthy of his genius than any he has yet written.

University Press: John Wilson & Son, Cambridge.